The
Stupidest
Angel

A

HEARTWARMING TALE

OF CHRISTMAS TERROR

A

HEARTWARMING TALE

OF CHRISTMAS TERROR

WILLIAM MORROW

An Imprint of HarperCollins*Publishers*

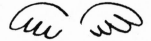

The
Stupidest
Angel

Christopher Moore

THE STUPIDEST ANGEL, VERSION 2.0. Copyright © 2004, 2005 by Christopher Moore. All rights reserved. Printed in the United States of America. No part of this book may be used or reproduced in any manner whatsoever without written permission except in the case of brief quotations embodied in critical articles and reviews. For information address HarperCollins Publishers, 10 East 53rd Street, New York, NY 10022.

HarperCollins books may be purchased for educational, business, or sales promotional use. For information please write: Special Markets Department, HarperCollins Publishers, 10 East 53rd Street, New York, NY 10022.

Designed by Betty Lew

Library of Congress Cataloging-in-Publication Data

Moore, Christopher, 1957–
    The stupidest angel : a heartwarming tale of Christmas terror / Christopher Moore.—1st ed.
      p. cm
    ISBN 0-06-059025-4 (hardcover)
    1. Seaside resorts—Fiction.   2. Community life—Fiction.
   3. Zombies—Fiction. I. Title.

PS3563.O594S78   2004
813'.54—dc22   2004049908

ISBN-13: 978-0-06-084235-2 (rev. ed.)
ISBN-10: 0-06-084235-0

06 07 08 09 WBC/QW 10 9 8 7 6 5 4 3 2

This book is dedicated to

who said:
"You know, you oughtta write a Christmas book."

To which I replied:
"What kind of Christmas book?"

To which he replied:
"I don't know. Maybe Christmas in Pine Cove
or something."

To which I replied:
" 'Kay."

Acknowledgments

The author wishes to acknowledge those who helped: as always, Nicholas Ellison, my intrepid agent; Jennifer Brehl, my brilliant editor; Lisa Gallagher and Michael Morrison for continued confidence in my ability to tell stories; Jack Womack and Leslie Cohen for getting me in front of my readers and the press; the Huffmans, for preparing a landing pad and a warm welcome; Charlee Rodgers, for the careful reads, thoughtful comments, and just putting up with the process; and finally, Taco Bob, from whom I joyfully (and with permission, which almost ruins it) swiped the idea for chapter 16.

Author's Warning

If you're buying this book as a gift for your grandma or a kid, you should be aware that it contains cusswords as well as tasteful depictions of cannibalism and people in their forties having sex. Don't blame me. I told you.

Chapter 1

CHRISTMAS CREEPS

Christmas crept into Pine Cove like a creeping Christmas thing: dragging garland, ribbon, and sleigh bells, oozing eggnog, reeking of pine, and threatening festive doom like a cold sore under the mistletoe.

Pine Cove, her pseudo-Tudor architecture all tarted up in holiday quaintage—twinkle lights in all the trees along Cypress Street, fake snow blown into the corner of every shop's windows, miniature Santas and giant candles hovering illuminated beneath every street-light—opened to the droves of tourists from Los Angeles, San Francisco, and the Central Valley searching for a truly meaningful moment of Christmas commerce. Pine Cove, sleepy California coastal village—a toy town, really, with more art galleries than gas stations, more wine-tasting rooms than hardware stores—lay there, as inviting as a drunken prom queen, as Christmas loomed, only five days away. Christmas was coming, and with Christmas this year, would come the Child. Both were vast and irresistible, and miraculous. Pine Cove was expecting only one of the two.

Which is not to say that the locals didn't get into the Christmas spirit. The two weeks before and after Christmas provided a welcome wave of cash into the town's coffers, tourist-starved since summer. Every waitress dusted off her Santa hat and clip-on reindeer antlers and checked to make sure that there were four good pens in her apron. Hotel clerks steeled themselves for the rage of last-minute overbookings, while house-keepers switched from their normal putrid baby-powder air fresheners to a more festive putrid pine and cinna-mon. Down at the Pine Cove Boutique they put a "Holiday Special" sign on the hideous reindeer sweater and marked it up for the tenth consecutive year. The Elks, Moose, Masons, and VFWs, who were basically the same bunch of drunk old guys, planned furiously for their annual Christmas parade down Cypress Street, the theme of which this year would be Patriotism in the Bed of a Pickup (mainly because that had been the theme of their Fourth of July parade and everyone still had the decorations). Many Pine Covers even volunteered to man the Salvation Army kettles down in front of the post office and the Thrifty-Mart in two-hour shifts, sixteen hours a day. Dressed in their red suits and fake beards, they rang their bells like they were going for dog-spit gold at the Pavlov Olympics.

"Give up the cash, you cheap son of a bitch," said Lena Marquez, who was working the kettle that Monday, five days before Christmas. Lena was following Dale Pearson, Pine Cove's evil developer, through the parking lot, ringing the bejeezus out of him as he headed for his truck. On his way into the Thrifty-Mart, he'd nodded to her and said, "Catch you on the way out," but when he emerged eight minutes later, carrying a sack of groceries and a bag of ice, he blew by her kettle like she was using it to render tallow from building inspectors' butts and he needed to escape the stench.

"It's not like you can't afford a couple of bucks for the less fortunate."

She rang her bell especially hard right by his ear and he spun around, swinging the bag of ice at her about hip level.

Lena jumped back. She was thirty-eight, lean, dark-skinned, with the delicate neck and finely set jawline of a flamenco dancer; her long black hair was coiled into two Princess Leia cinnabuns on either side of her Santa hat. "You can't take a swing at Santa! That's wrong in so many ways that I don't have time to enumerate them."

"You mean to *count* them," Dale said, the soft winter sunlight glinting off a new set of veneers he'd just had installed on his front teeth. He was fifty-two, almost completely bald, and had strong carpenter's shoulders that were still wide and square, despite the beer gut hanging below.

"I mean it's wrong—you're wrong—and you're cheap," and with that Lena put the bell next to his ear again and shook it like a red-suited terrier shaking the life out of a screaming brass rat.

Dale cringed at the sound and swung the ten-pound bag of ice in a great underhanded arc that caught Lena in the solar plexus and sent her backpedaling across the parking lot, gasping for breath. That's when the ladies at BULGES called the cops—well, cop.

BULGES was a women's fitness center located just above the parking lot of the Thrifty-Mart, and from their treadmills and stair-climbing machines, the BULGES members could watch the ins and outs of the local market without feeling as if they were actively spying. So what had started as a moment of sheer glee and a mild adrenaline surge for the six of them who were watching as Lena chased Dale through the parking lot, turned quickly to shock as the evil developer thwacked the Latin Santa-ette in the breadbasket with a satchel of minicubes. Five of the six merely missed a step or gasped, but Georgia Bauman—who had her treadmill cranked up to eight miles per hour at that very moment, because she was trying to lose fifteen pounds by Christmas and fit into a red-sequined sheath cocktail dress her husband had bought for her in a fit of sexual idealism—bowled backward off her treadmill and landed in a colorful spandex tangle of yoga students who had been practicing on the mats behind her.

"Ow, my ass chakra!"

"That's you're root chakra."

"Feels like my ass."

"Did you see that? He nearly knocked her off her feet. Poor thing."

"Should we see if she's all right?"

"Someone should call Theo."

The exercisers opened their cell phones in unison, like the Jets flicking switchblades as they gaily danced into a *West Side Story* gang-fight to the death.

"Why did she ever marry that guy, anyway?"

"He's such an asshole."

"She used to drink."

"Georgia, are you all right, honey?"

"Can you get Theo by calling 911?"

"That bastard is just going to drive off and leave her there."

"We should go help."

"I've got twelve more minutes on this thing."

"The cell reception in this town is horrible."

"I have Theo's number on speed dial, for the kids. Let me call."

"Look at Georgia and the girls. It looks like they were playing Twister and fell."

"Hello, Theo. This is Jane down at BULGES. Yes, well, I just glanced out the window here and I noticed that there might be a problem over at the Thrifty-Mart. Well, I don't want to meddle, but let's just say that a certain contractor just hit one of the Salvation Army Santas with a bag of ice. Well, I'll look for your car, then." She flipped the phone shut. "He's on his way."

Theophilus Crowe's mobile phone played eight bars of "Tangled Up in Blue" in an irritating electronic voice that sounded like a choir of suffering houseflies, or Jiminy Cricket huffing helium, or, well, you know, Bob Dylan—anyway, by the time he got the device open, five people in the produce section of the Thrifty-Mart were giving him the hairy eyeball hard enough to wilt the arugula right there in his cart. He grinned as if to say,

Sorry, I hate these things, too, but what are you gonna do? then he answered, "Constable Crowe," just to remind everyone that he wasn't dicking around here, he was THE LAW.

"In the parking lot of the Thrifty-Mart? Okay, I'll be right there."

Wow, this was convenient. One thing about being the resident lawman in a town of only five thousand people—you were never far from the trouble. Theo parked his cart on the end of the aisle and loped by the registers and out the automatic doors to the parking lot. (He was a denim- and flannel-clad praying mantis of a man, six-six, one-eighty, and he only had three speeds: amble, lope, and still.) Outside he found Lena Marquez doubled over and gasping for breath. Her ex-husband, Dale Pearson, was stepping into his four-wheel-drive pickup.

"Right there, Dale. Wait," Theo said.

Theo ascertained that Lena had only had the wind knocked out of her and was going to be okay, then addressed the stocky contractor, who had paused with one boot on the running board, as if he'd be on his way as soon as the hot air cleared out of the truck.

"What happened here?"

"The crazy bitch hit me with that bell of hers."

"Did not," gasped Lena.

"I got a report you hit her with a bag of ice, Dale. That's assault."

Dale Pearson looked around quickly and spotted the crowd of women gathered by the window over at the gym. They all looked away, heading for the various machines they had been on when the debacle unfolded. "Ask them. They'll tell you she had that bell right upside my head. I just reacted out of self-defense."

"He said he'd donate when he came out of the store, then he didn't," Lena said, her breath coming back. "There's an implied contract there. He violated it. And I didn't hit him."

"She's a fucking nutcase." Dale said it like he was declaring water wet—like it was just understood.

Theo looked from one of them to the other. He'd dealt with these two before, but thought it had all come to rest when they'd divorced five years ago. (He'd been constable of Pine Cove for fourteen years—he'd seen the wrong side of a lot of couples.) First rule in a domestic situation was separate the parties, but that appeared to have already been accomplished. You weren't supposed to take sides, but since Theo had a soft spot for nutcases—he'd married one himself—he decided to make a judgment call and focus his attention on Dale. Besides, the guy was an asshole.

Theo patted Lena's back and loped over to Dale's truck.

"Don't waste your time, hippie," Dale said. "I'm done." He climbed into his truck and closed the door.

Hippie? Theo thought. *Hippie?* He'd cut his ponytail years ago. He'd stopped wearing Birkenstocks. He'd even stopped smoking pot. Where did this guy get off calling him a hippie?

Hippie? he said to himself, then: "Hey!"

Dale started his truck and put it into gear.

Theo stepped up on the running board, leaned over the windshield, and started tapping on it with a quarter he'd fished from his jeans pocket. "Don't leave, Dale." *Tap, tap, tap.* "You leave now, I'll put a warrant out for your arrest." *Tap, tap, tap.* Theo was pissed now—he was sure of it. Yes, this was definitely anger now.

Dale threw the truck into park and hit the electric window button. "What? What do you want?"

"Lena wants to press charges for assault—maybe assault with a deadly weapon. I think you'd better rethink leaving right now."

"Deadly weapon? It was a bag of ice."

Theo shook his head, affected a whimsical storyteller's tone: "A ten-pound bag of ice. Listen, Dale, as I drop a *ten-pound* block of ice on the courtroom floor in front of the jury. Can you hear it? Can't you just see the jury cringe as I smash a honeydew melon on the defense attorney's table with a *ten-pound* block of ice? Not a deadly weapon? 'Ladies and gentlemen of the jury, this man, this reprobate, this redneck, this—if I may—clump-filled-cat-box-of-a-man, struck a defenseless woman—a woman who out of the kindness of her heart was collecting for the poor, a woman who was only—"

"But it's not a block of ice, it's—"

Theo raised a finger in the air. "Not another word, Dale, not until I read you your rights." Theo could tell he was getting to Dale—veins were starting to pulse in the contractor's temples and his bald head was turning bright pink. *Hippie, huh?* "Lena is definitely pressing charges, aren't you, Lena?"

Lena had made her way to the side of the truck.

"No," Lena said.

"Bitch!" Theo said—it slipped out before he could stop himself. He'd been on such a roll.

"See how she is," said Dale. "Wish you had a bag of ice now, don't you, hippie?"

"I'm an officer of the law," Theo said, wishing he had a gun or something. He pulled his badge wallet out of his back pocket but decided that was a little late for ID, since he'd known Dale for nearly twenty years.

"Yeah, and I'm a Caribou," Dale said, with more pride than he really should have had about that.

"I'll forget all about it if he puts a hundred bucks in the kettle," Lena said.

"You're nuts, woman."

"It's Christmas, Dale."

"Fuck Christmas and fuck you."

"Hey, there's no need for that kind of talk, Dale," Theo said, going for the *peace* in peace officer. "You can just step out of the truck."

"Fifty bucks in the kettle and he can go," Lena said. "It's for the needy."

Theo whipped around and looked at her. "You can't plea-bargain in the parking lot of the Thrifty-Mart. I had him on the ropes."

"Shut up, hippie," Dale said. Then to Lena, "You'll take twenty and the needy can get bent. They can get a job like the rest of us."

Theo was sure he had handcuffs in the Volvo—or were they still on the bedpost at home? "That is not the way we—"

"Forty!" Lena shouted.

"Done!" Dale said. He pulled two twenties from his wallet, wadded them up, and threw them out the window so they bounced off of Theo Crowe's chest. He threw the truck in gear and backed out.

"Stop right there!" Theo commanded.

Dale righted the truck and took off. As the big red pickup passed Theo's Volvo station wagon, parked twenty yards up the lot, a bag of ice came flying out the window and exploded against the Volvo's tailgate, showering the parking lot with cubes but otherwise doing no damage whatsoever. "Merry Christmas, you psycho bitch!" Dale shouted out the window as he turned onto the street. "And to all a good night! Hippie!"

Lena had tucked the wadded bills into her Santa suit and was squeezing Theo's shoulder as the red truck roared out of sight. "Thanks for coming to my rescue, Theo."

"Not much of a rescue. You should press charges."

"I'm okay. He'd have gotten out of it anyway; he has great lawyers. Trust me, I know. Besides, forty bucks!"

"That's the Christmas spirit," Theo said, not able to keep from smiling. "You sure you're okay?"

"I'm fine. It's not the first time he's lost it with me." She patted the pocket of her Santa suit. "At least something came of this." She started back to her kettle and Theo followed.

"You have a week to file charges if you change your mind," Theo said.

"You know what, Theo? I really don't want to spend another Christmas obsessing on what a complete waste of humanity Dale Pearson is. I'd rather let it go. Maybe if we're lucky he'll be one of those holiday fatalities we're always hearing about."

"That would be nice," said Theo.

"Now who's in the Christmas spirit?"

In another Christmas story, Dale Pearson, evil developer, self-absorbed woman hater, and seemingly unredeemable curmudgeon, might be visited in the night by a series of ghosts who, by showing him bleak visions of Christmas future, past, and present, would bring about in him a change to generosity, kindness, and a general warmth toward his fellow man. But this is not that kind of Christmas story, so here, in not too many pages, someone is going to dispatch the miserable son of a bitch with a shovel. That's the spirit of Christmas yet to come in these parts. Ho, ho, ho.

Chapter 2

THE LOCAL GIRLS HAVE
A WAY ABOUT THEM

The Warrior Babe of the Outland steered her Honda station wagon down Cypress Street, stopping every ten feet or so for tourists who were stepping into the street from between parked cars, completely oblivious of any automobile traffic. *My kingdom for a razor-blade cowcatcher and Cuisinart wheel covers to cut my path through this herd of ignorant peasant meat,* she thought. Then: *Whoa, I guess I really do need the meds.* So she said, "They act like Cypress Street is the midway at Disneyland—like no one actually has to use the street to drive on. You guys wouldn't do that, would you?"

She glanced over her shoulder at the two damp teenage boys who were huddled in the corner of the backseat of the car. They shook their heads furiously. One said, "No, Miss Michon, no we'd never. No."

Her real name was Molly Michon, but years ago, as a B-movie queen, she'd done eight movies as Kendra, Warrior Babe of the Outland. She had a wild mane of blond hair shot with gray and the body of a fitness model. She could pass for thirty or fifty, depending on the time of day, what she was wearing, and how deeply medicated she was. Fans agreed that she was probably somewhere in her early to midforties.

Fans. The two teenage boys in the backseat of the car were fans. They'd made the mistake of taking part of their Christmas break to go to Pine Cove in search of the famed cult-film star, Molly Michon, and get her autograph on their copies of *Warrior Babe VI: Revenge of the Savage Skank,* just released on DVD, with never-before-seen outtakes of Molly's boobs popping out of her gunmetal bra. Molly had seen them skulking around the outside of the cabin she shared with her husband, Theo Crowe. She'd snuck out the back door and ambushed them on the side of the house with a garden hose— sprayed them down good, chased them through the pine forest till the hose reeled out of its cart, then she tackled the taller one and threatened to snap his neck if the other one didn't stop in his tracks.

Realizing at that point that she might have made a public relations error, Molly invited her fans to come

along to help pick out a Christmas tree for the Santa
Rosa Chapel Christmas Party for the Lonesome. (She
had been making more than a few minor misjudgments
lately, as she'd stopped taking her meds a week ago in
order to save money for Theo's Christmas present.)

"So, where are you guys from?" she said cheerfully.

"Please don't hurt us," said Bert, the taller, thinner
of the two kids. (She had been thinking of them as Bert
and Ernie—not because they really looked like the pup-
pets, but because they had the same relative shapes—
except for the big hand up their bottoms, of course.)

"I'm not going to hurt you. It's great to have you
along. The guys at the Christmas-tree lot are a little
wary of me since I fed one of their coworkers to a sea
monster a few years ago, so you guys can sort of act as a
social buffer." *Damn,* she shouldn't have mentioned the
sea monster. She'd had so many years of obscurity between the time she'd been pushed out of the movie
business until the revival to cult status of her movies that
she'd lost most of her people skills. And then there was
that fifteen-year disconnect with reality when she'd
been known as Pine Cove's crazy lady—but since she'd
hooked up with Theo, and had stayed on her antipsychotics, things had been a lot better.

She turned into the parking lot of Pine Cove Hardware and Gift, where a half acre of tarmac was corralled
off for the Christmas-tree lot. Upon spotting her car,

three middle-aged guys in canvas aprons quickstepped their way into the store, threw the bolt, and turned the "Open" sign to CLOSED.

She'd thought this might happen, but she wanted to surprise Theo, prove that she could handle getting the big Christmas tree for the chapel party. Now these narrow-minded minions of Black & Decker were foiling her plans for a perfect Christmas. She took a deep breath and tried to exhale herself into a calm moment as her yoga teacher had instructed.

Well, she did live in the middle of a pine forest, didn't she? Maybe she should just go cut a Christmas tree herself.

"Let's just go back to the cabin, guys. I have an ax there that will work."

"Noooooooo!" screamed Ernie as he reached across his damp friend, threw the latch on the Honda's door, and rolled them both out of the moving car into a pallet of plastic reindeer.

"Okay, then," Molly said, "you guys take care. I'll just see if I can cut a tree out of the front yard." She swung around in the parking lot and headed back home.

Slick with sweat, Lena Marquez slid out of her Santa suit like a baby lizard emerging from a fuzzy red egg. The temperature had risen into the high seventies before she'd finished her shift at the Thrifty-Mart, and she was sure she'd probably lost five pounds in water in the heavy suit. Wearing only her bra and panties, she padded into the bathroom and jumped on the scale to enjoy the surprise bonus weight loss. The disk spun and settled on her usual preshower weight. Perfect for her height, light for her age, but dammit, she'd fought with her ex, been pounded with ice, rang out good cheer for the less fortunate, and endured the jolly heat of the Santa suit for eight hours, she deserved something for her efforts.

She took off her bra and panties and hopped back on the scale. No discernible difference. Dammit! She sat, peed, wiped, and jumped back on the scale. Maybe a third of a pound below normal. *Ah!* she thought, brushing her beard aside so she could read the scale more clearly, this could be the problem. She pulled off the white beard and Santa hat, flung them into the nearby bedroom, shook out her long black hair, and waited for the scale to settle.

Oh yeah. Four pounds. She did a quick Tae Bo kick of celebration and stepped into the shower. She winced as she soaped up, hitting a sore spot there by her solar plexus. There were a couple of purple bruises developing on her ribs where the ice bag had hit her. She'd had more pain after doing too many crunches at the gym, but this pain seemed to shoot on through to her heart. Maybe it was the thought of spending Christmas alone.

This would be her first since the divorce. Her sister, whom she'd spent the last few Christmases with, was going with her husband and the kids to Europe. Dale, total prick that he was, had involved her in all sorts of holiday activities from which she was now excluded. The rest of her family was back in Chicago, and she hadn't had any luck with men since Dale—too much residual anger and mistrust. (He hadn't just been a prick, he had cheated on her.) Her girlfriends, all of them married or paired up with semipermanent boy-friends, told her that she needed to be single for a while, spend some time getting to know herself. That, of course, was total bullshit. She knew herself, liked herself, washed herself, dressed herself, bought herself presents, took herself out on dates, and even had sex with herself from time to time, which always ended better than it used to with Dale.

"Oh, that get-to-know-yourself stuff will send you full-blown batshit," said her friend Molly Michon. "And believe me, I am the uncrowned queen of batshit. Last time I really got to know myself it turned out there was a whole gang of bitches in there to deal with. I felt like the receptionist at a rehab center. They all had nice tits, though, I gotta say. Anyway, forget that. Go out and do stuff for someone else. That's much better for you. 'Get to know yourself'—what good is that? What if you get to know yourself and find out you're a total harpy?

Sure, I like you, but you can't trust my judgment. Go do something for other people."

It was true. Molly could be—uh, eccentric, but she did make sense occasionally. So Lena had volunteered to man the Salvation Army kettle, she'd collected canned food and frozen turkeys for the Pine Cove Anonymous Neighbors food drive, and tomorrow night, as soon as it got dark, she was going to go out and collect live Christmas trees and drop them off at the homes of people who probably wouldn't be able to afford them. That should take her mind off herself. And if it didn't work, she'd spend Christmas Eve at the Santa Rosa Chapel Party for the Lonesome. Oh God, there it was. It was Christmastime, and she was in the Christmas spirit—she was feeling lonesome . . .

To Mavis Sand, the owner of the Head of the Slug saloon, the word *lonesome* rang like the bell on a cash register. Come Christmas break, Pine Cove filled up with tourists seeking small-town charm, and the Head of the Slug filled up with lonesome, disenfranchised whiners seeking solace. Mavis was glad to serve it up in the form of her signature (and overpriced) Christmas cocktail: the Slow Comfortable Screw in the Back of Santa's Sleigh, which consisted of—"Well, fuck off if you need to know what's in it," Mavis would say. "I'm a professional bartender since your daddy flushed the condom that held your only hope of havin' a brain, so get in the spirit and order the goddamn drink."

Mavis was always in the Christmas spirit, right down to the Christmas-tree earrings that she wore year-round to give her that "new-car smell." A sheaf of mistletoe the size of a moose head hung over the order station at her bar, and throughout the season, any unsuspecting drunk who leaned too far over the bar to shout his order into one of Mavis's hearing aids would find that beyond the fluttering black nylon whips of her mascara-plastered pseudo lashes, behind the mole with the hair and the palette knife–applied cakes of Red Seduction lipstick, past the Tareyton 100s breath and the clacking dentures, Mavis still had some respectable tongue action left in her. One guy, breathless and staggering toward the door, claimed that she had tongued his medulla oblongata and stimulated visions of being choked in Death's dark closet—which Mavis took as a compliment.

About the same time that Dale and Lena were having their go-round down at the Thrifty-Mart, Mavis, perched on her stool behind the bar, looked up from a crossword puzzle to see the most beautiful man she'd ever lain eyes on coming through Slug's double doors. What had once been a desert bloomed down under; where for years lay a dusty streambed, a mighty river did now flow. Her heart skipped a beat and the defibrillator implanted in her chest gave her a little jolt that sent her sluicing electric off her bar stool to his service. If he ordered a wallbanger she'd come so hard her tennis shoes would rip out from the toe curl, she knew it, she felt it, she wanted it. Mavis was a romantic.

"Can I help you?" she asked, batting her eyelashes, which gave the appearance of spastic wolf spiders convulsing behind her glasses.

A half-dozen daytime regulars who had been sitting at the bar turned on their stools to behold the source of that oily courtesy—there was no way that voice had come out of Mavis, who normally spoke to them in tones of disdain and nicotine.

"I'm looking for a child," said the stranger. He had long blond hair that fanned out over the rain flap of a black trench coat. His eyes were violet, his facial features both rugged and delicate, finely cut and yet with no lines of age or experience.

Mavis tweaked the little knob on her right hearing aid and tilted her head like a dog who has just bitten into a plastic pork chop. Oh, how the pillars of lust can crumble under the weight of stupidity. "You're looking for a *child*?" asked Mavis.

"Yes," said the stranger.

"In a bar? On a Monday afternoon? You're looking for a child?"

"Yes."

"A particular child, or will just any child do?"

"I'll know it when I see it," said the stranger.

"You sick fuck," said one of the daytime regulars, and Mavis, for once, nodded in agreement, her neck vertebrae clicking like a socket wrench.

"Get the hell out of my bar," she said. A long, lacquered fingernail pointed the way back out the door. "Go on, get out. What do you think this is, Bangkok?"

The stranger looked at her finger. "The Nativity is approaching, am I correct?"

"Yeah, Christmas is Saturday," Mavis growled. "The hell does that have anything to do with anything?"

"Then I'll need a child before Saturday," said the stranger.

Mavis reached under the bar and pulled out her miniature baseball bat. Just because he was pretty didn't mean he couldn't be improved by a smack upside the head with a piece of earnest hickory. Men: a wink, a thrill, a damp squish, and before you knew it it was time to start raising lumps and loosening teeth. Mavis was a pragmatic romantic: love—correctly performed, she believed—hurts.

"Smack 'im, Mavis," cheered one of the daytime regulars.

"What kind of perv wears an overcoat in seventy-five-degree weather?" said another. "I say brain him."

Bets were beginning to be exchanged back by the pool table.

Mavis tugged at an errant chin hair and peered over her glasses at the stranger. "Think you might want to move your little search on down the road some?"

"What day is it?" asked the stranger.

"Monday."

"Then I'll have a diet Coke."

"What about the kid?" asked Mavis, punctuating the question by smacking the baseball bat against her palm (which hurt like hell, but she wasn't going to flinch, not a chance).

"I have until Saturday," said the beautiful perv. "For now, just a diet Coke—and a Snickers bar. Please."

"That's it," Mavis said. "You're a dead man."

"But, I said *please*," said Blondie, missing the point, somewhat.

She didn't even bother to throw open the lift-away through the bar but ducked under it and charged. At that moment a bell rang, and a beam of light blasted into the bar, indicating that someone had come in from outside. When Mavis stood back up, leaning heavily on her back foot as she wound up to knock the stranger's nads well into the next county, he was gone.

"Problem, Mavis?" asked Theophilus Crowe. The constable was standing right where the stranger had been.

"Damn, where'd he go?" Mavis looked around behind Theo, then back at the daytime regulars.

"Where'd he go?"

"Got me," they said, a chorus of shrugs.

"Who?" asked Theo.

"Blond guy in a black trench coat," said Mavis. "You had to pass him on the way in."

"Trench coat? It's seventy-five degrees out," said Theo. "I'd have noticed someone in a trench coat."

"He was a perv!" someone shouted from the back.

Theo looked down at Mavis. "This guy flash you?"

Their height difference was nearly two feet and Mavis had to back up a step to look him in the eye. "Hell no. I like a man who believes in truth in advertising. This guy was looking for a child."

"He told you that? He came in here and said he was looking for a kid?"

"That's it. I was just getting ready to teach him some—"

"You're sure he hadn't lost *his* kid? That happens, Christmas shopping, they wander away—"

"No, he wasn't looking for a particular kid, he was just looking for *a* kid."

"Well, maybe he wanted to be a Big Brother or Secret Santa or something," said Theo, expressing a faith in the goodness of man for which he had little to no evidence, "do something nice for Christmas."

"Goddammit, Theo, you dumbfuck, you don't have to pry a priest off an altar boy with a crowbar to figure out that he's not helping the kid with his Rosary. The guy was a perv."

"Well, I should probably go look for him."

"Well, you probably oughta should."

Theo started to turn to go out the door, then turned back. "I'm not a dumbfuck, Mavis. There's no need for that kind of talk."

"Sorry, Theo," said Mavis, lowering her baseball bat to show the sincerity of her contrition. "Why was it you came in, then?"

"Can't remember." Theo raised his eyebrows, daring her.

Mavis grinned at him. Theo was a good guy—a little flaky but a good guy. "Really?"

"Nah, I just wanted to check with you on the food for the Christmas party. You were going to barbecue, right?"

"I was planning on it."

"Well, I just heard on the radio that there's a pretty good chance of rain, so you might want to have a backup plan."

"More liquor?"

"I was thinking something that wouldn't involve cooking outdoors."

"Like more liquor?"

Theo shook his head and started toward the door. "Call me or Molly if you need any help."

"It won't rain," said Mavis. "It never rains in December."

But Theo was gone, out on the street looking for the trench-coated stranger.

"It could rain," said one of the daytime regulars. "Scientists say we could see El Niño this year."

"Yeah, like they ever tell us until after half the state has washed away," said Mavis. "Screw the scientists."

But El Niño *was* coming.

El Niño. The Child.

Chapter 3

HOSED FOR THE HOLIDAYS

Tuesday night. Christmas was still four days away, and yet there was Santa Claus cruising right down the main street of town in his big red pickup truck: waving to the kids, weaving in his lane, belching into his beard, more than a little drunk. "Ho, ho, ho," said Dale Pearson, evil developer and Caribou Lodge Santa for the sixth consecutive year. "Ho, ho, ho," he said, suppressing the urge to add *and a bottle of rum,* his demeanor more akin to that of Blackbeard than Saint Nicholas. Parents pointed, children waved and frisked.

By now, all of Pine Cove was abuzz with expat Christmas cheer. Every hotel room was full, and there wasn't a parking space to be found down on Cypress Street, where shoppers pumped their chestnuts into an open fire of credit-card swipe-and-spend denial. It smelled of cinnamon and pine, peppermint and joy. This was not the coarse commercialism of a Los Angeles or San Francisco Christmas. This was the refined, sincere commercialism of small-town New England, where a century ago Norman Rockwell had invented Christmas. This was real.

But Dale didn't get it. "Merry, happy—oh, eat me, you little vermin," Dale grinched from behind his tinted windows.

Actually, the whole Christmas appeal of their village was a bit of a mystery to the residents of Pine Cove. It wasn't exactly a winter wonderland; the median temperature in the winter was sixty-five degrees Fahrenheit, and only a couple of really old guys could remember it ever having snowed. Neither was it a tropical-beach getaway. The ocean there was bitterly cold, with an average visibility of eighteen inches, and a huge elephant seal rookery at the shore. Through the winter thousands of the rotund pinnipeds lay strewn across Pine Cove beaches like great barking turds, and although not dangerous in themselves, they were the dietary mainstay of the great white shark, which had evolved over 120 million years into the perfect excuse for never entering water over one's ankles. So if it wasn't the weather or the water, what in the hell was it? Perhaps it was the pine trees themselves. Christmas trees.

"My trees, goddammit," Dale grumbled to himself.

Pine Cove lay in the last natural Monterey-pine forest in the world. Because they grow as much as twenty feet a year, Monterey pines are the very trees cultivated for Christmas trees. The good news was you could go to almost any undeveloped lot in town and cut yourself a very respectable Christmas tree. The bad news was that it was a crime to do so unless you obtained a permit and planted five trees to replace it. The Monterey pines were a protected species, as any local builder could tell you, because whenever they cut down a few trees to build a home, they had to plant a forest to replace them.

A station wagon with a Christmas tree lashed to the roof backed out in front of Dale's pickup. "Get that piece of shit off my street," Dale scrooged. "And Merry Christmas to all you scumbags," he added, in keeping with the season.

Dale Pearson, quite unwillingly, had become the Johnny Appleseed of the Christmas tree, having planted tens of thousands of seedlings to replace the thousands that he had chain-sawed to build rows of tract mansions across Pine Cove's hills. But while the law stated that the replacement trees had to be planted within the municipality of Pine Cove, it didn't say that they had to go in anywhere near where they had actually been cut down, so Dale planted all of his trees around the cemetery at the old Santa Rosa Chapel. He'd bought the land, ten acres, years ago, in hope of subdividing it and building luxury homes, but some hippie meddlers from the California Historical Society stepped in and had the old two-room chapel declared a historic landmark, thus making it impossible for him to develop his land. So in straight rows, with no thought for the natural lay of a forest, his construction crews planted Monterey pines until the trees became as thick around the chapel as feathers on a bird's back.

For the last four years, during the week before Christmas, someone had gone onto Dale's land and dug up truckloads of live pine trees. He was tired of answering to the county about having to replace them. He didn't give a damn about the trees, but he'd be damned if he'd put up with someone siccing the county watchdogs on him over and over. He'd fulfilled his duty to his Caribou buddies of passing out joke gifts to them and their wives, but now he was going to catch a thief. His Christmas present this year was going to be a little justice. That's all he wanted, just a little justice.

The jolly old elf turned off Cypress and headed up

the hill toward the chapel, patting the thirty-eight snub-
nose revolver he'd stuffed into his wide black belt.

Lena hefted the second Christmas tree into the bed of
her little Toyota pickup and snuggled it into one of the
ten-gallon cedar boxes that she'd nailed together herself
just for that purpose. The underprivileged were only
getting four-footers this year, maybe a foot or so taller
once in the box. It had rained only once since October,
so it had taken her nearly an hour and a half to dig the
two saplings from the hard, dry ground. She wanted
people to have live Christmas trees, but if she went for
full seven-footers she'd be out here all night and only
get a couple. *This is real work,* Lena thought. By day she
did property management for vacation rentals at a local
realtor, sometimes putting in ten- or twelve-hour days
during the peak seasons, but she realized that hours
spent and actual work were two different things. She realized it every year when she came out here by herself
and got behind her bright red shovel.

Sweat was pouring down her face. She wiped her
hair out of her eyes with the back of a chamois work
glove, leaving a streak of dirt on her forehead. She
shrugged off the flannel shirt she'd put on against the
night chill and worked in a tight black tank top and
olive drab cargo pants. With her red shovel in hand, she

looked like some kind of Christmas commando there at the edge of the forest.

She sank the shovel into the pine straw about a foot from the trunk of the next tree she'd targeted and jumped on the blade, pogoing up and down until the blade was buried to the hilt. She was swinging on the handle, trying to lever up the forest floor, when a bright set of headlights swept across the edge of the forest and stopped with a stereo spotlight on Lena's truck.

There's nothing to worry about, she thought. *I'm not going to hide, I'm not going to duck.* She wasn't doing anything wrong. Not really. Well, sure, technically, she was stealing, and breaking a couple of county ordinances about harvesting Monterey pines, but she wasn't really harvesting them, was she? She was just transplanting them. And . . . and she was giving to the poor. She was like Robin Hood. No one was going to mess with Robin Hood. Just the same she smiled at the headlamps and did a sort of "oh well, I guess I'm busted" shrug that she hoped was cute. She shielded her eyes with her hand and tried to squint into the headlights to see who was driving the truck. Yes, she was sure it was a truck.

The engine sputtered to a stop. A slight nausea rose in Lena's throat as she realized that it was a diesel truck. The truck's door opened, and when the light went on Lena caught a glimpse of someone in a red-and-white hat behind the wheel.

Huh?

Santa was coming out of the blinding light toward her. Santa with a flashlight, and what was that in his belt? Santa had a gun.

"Dammit, Lena, I should have known it was you," he said.

Josh Barker was in big trouble. Big trouble indeed. He was only seven, but he was pretty sure his life was ruined. He hurried along Church Street trying to figure out how he was going to explain to his mom. An hour and a half late. Home long after dark. And he hadn't called. And Christmas just a few days away. Forget explaining it to his mom, how was he going to explain it to Santa?

Santa might understand, though, since he knew toys. But Mom would never buy it. He'd been playing *Barbarian George's Big Crusade* on the PlayStation at his friend Sam's house, and they'd gotten into the infidel territory and killed thousands of the 'Rackies, but the game just didn't have any way to exit. It wasn't designed so you could ever get out of it, and before he knew it, it was dark outside and he'd forgotten, and Christmas was just going to be ruined. He wanted an Xbox 2, but there was no way Santa was going to bring it with a *home long after dark* AND a *didn't even bother to call* on his list.

Sam had summarized Josh's situation as he led him out the door and looked at the night sky: "Dude, you're hosed."

"I'm not hosed, you're hosed," said Josh.

"I'm not hosed," Sam said. "I'm Jewish. No Santa. We don't have Christmas."

"Well, you're really hosed, then."

"Shut up, I am not hosed." But as Sam said it he put his hands in his pockets and Josh could hear him clicking his dreidel against his asthma inhaler, and his friend did, indeed, appear to be hosed.

"Okay, you're not hosed," said Josh. "Sorry. I'd better go."

"Yeah," said Sam.

"Yeah," said Josh, realizing now how the longer it took him to get home the more hosed he was going to be. But as he hurried up Church Street toward home, he realized that perhaps he would receive an emergency reprieve on his hosing, for there, at the edge of the forest, was Santa himself. And although Santa did appear to be quite angry, his anger was directed at a woman who was standing knee-deep in a hole, holding a red shovel. Santa held one of those heavy black Maglite flashlights in one hand and was shining it in the woman's eyes as he yelled at her.

"These are my trees. Mine, dammit," said Santa.

Aha! Josh thought. *Dammit was not bad enough to*

get you on the naughty list, not if Santa himself said it. He'd told his mom that, but she'd insisted that *dammit* was a list item.

"I'm only taking a few," said the woman. "For people who can't afford a Christmas tree. You can't begrudge something that simple to a few poor families."

"The fuck I can't."

Well, Josh had been sure the F-word would get you on the list. He was shocked.

Santa pushed the flashlight in the woman's eyes. She brushed it aside.

"Look," she said, "I'll just take this last one and go."

"You will not." Santa shoved the flashlight in the woman's face again, but this time when she brushed it away, he flipped it around and bopped her on the head with it.

"Ouch!"

That had to hurt. Josh could feel the blow rattle the woman's teeth all the way across the street. Santa certainly felt strongly about his Christmas trees.

The woman used the shovel to brush the flashlight out of her face again. Santa bopped her again with the flashlight, harder this time, and the woman yowled and fell to her knees in the hole. Santa reached into his big black belt and pulled out a gun and pointed it at the woman. She came up swinging the shovel in a wide arc and the blade caught Santa hard in the side of the head with a dull metallic clank. Santa staggered and raised the pistol again. The woman crouched and covered her head, the shovel braced blade up under her arm. But as he aimed, Santa lost his balance, and fell forward onto the upraised blade of the shovel. The blade went up under his beard and suddenly his beard was as bright red as his suit. He dropped the gun and the flashlight, made a gurgling noise, and fell down to where Josh could no longer see him.

Josh could barely hear the woman crying as he ran home, the pulse in his ears ringing like sleigh bells. Santa was dead. Christmas was ruined. Josh was hosed.

Speaking of hosed: three blocks away, Tucker Case moped along Worchester Street, trying to exercise off his dinner of bad diner food with a brisk walk under the weight of a large measure of self-pity. He was pushing forty, trim, blond, and tan—the look of an aging surfer or a golf pro in his prime. Fifty feet above him, a giant fruit bat swooped through the treetops, his leathery wings silent against the night. So he could sneak up on peaches and stuff without being detected, Tuck thought.

"Roberto, do your business and let's get back to the hotel," Tuck called into the sky. The fruit bat barked and snagged an overhead limb as he passed, his momentum nearly sending him in a loop around it before he pendulumed and settled in upside-down attitude. The bat barked again, licked his little doggy chops, and folded his great wings around himself to ward off the coastal cold.

"Fine," Tuck said, "but you're not getting back into the room until you poop."

He'd inherited the bat from a Filipino navigator he'd met while flying a private jet for a doctor in Micronesia; a job he'd only taken because his U.S. pilot's license had been yanked for crashing the pink Mary Jean Cosmetic jet while initiating a young woman into the Mile-High Club. Drunk. After Micronesia he'd moved to the Caribbean with his fruit bat and his beautiful new island wife and started a charter business. Now, six years later, his beautiful island wife was running the charter business with a seven-foot Rastafarian and Tucker Case had nothing to his name but a fruit bat and temporary gig flying helicopters for the DEA, spotting marijuana patches in the Big Sur wilderness area. Which put him in Pine Cove, holed up in a cheap motel room, four days before Christmas, alone. Lonesome. Hosed.

Tuck had once been a ladies' man of the highest order—a Don Juan, a Casanova, a Kennedy sans cash— yet now he was in a town where he didn't know a soul and he hadn't even met a single woman to try to seduce.

A few years of marriage had almost ruined him. He'd become accustomed to affectionate female company without a great deal of manipulation, subterfuge, and guile. He missed it. He didn't want to spend Christmas alone, dammit. Yet here he was.

And there she was. A damsel in distress. A woman, alone, out here in the night, crying—and from what Tuck could tell by the headlights of a nearby pickup truck, she had a nice shape. Great hair. Beautiful high cheekbones, streaked with tears and mud, but you know, exotic-looking. Tuck checked to see that Roberto was still safely hanging above, then straightened his bomber jacket and made his way across the street.

"Hey there, are you okay?"

The woman jumped, screamed a bit, looked around frantically until she spotted him. "Oh my God," she said.

Tuck had had worse responses. He pressed on. "Are you okay?" he repeated. "You looked like you were having some trouble."

"I think he's dead," the woman said. "I think—I think I killed him."

Tuck looked at the red-and-white pile on the ground at his feet and realized for the first time what it really was: a dead Santa. A normal person might have freaked out, backed away, tried to quickly extract himself from the situation, but Tucker Case was a pilot, trained to function in life-and-death emergencies, practiced at grace under pressure, and besides, he was lonely and this woman was really hot.

"So, a dead Santa," said Tuck. "Do you live around here?"

"I didn't mean to kill him. He was coming at me with a gun. I just ducked, and when I looked up—" She waved toward the pile of dead Kringle. "I guess the shovel caught him in the throat." She seemed to be calming down a bit.

Tuck nodded thoughtfully. "So, Santa was coming at you with a gun?"

The woman pointed to the gun, lying in the dirt next to the Maglite. "I see," said Tuck. "Did you know this—"

"Yes. His name is Dale Pearson. He drank."

"I don't. Stopped years ago," Tuck said. "By the way, I'm Tucker Case. Are you married?" He extended his hand to her to shake. She seemed to see him for the first time.

"Lena Marquez. No, I'm divorced."

"Me, too," said Tuck. "Tough around the holidays, isn't it? Kids?"

"No. Mr., uh, Case, this man is my ex-husband and he's dead."

"Yep. I just gave my ex the house and my business, but this does seems cheaper," Tuck said.

"We had a fight yesterday at the grocery store in front of a dozen people. I had the motive, the opportunity, and the means—" She pointed to the shovel. "Everyone will think I killed him."

"Not to mention that you did kill him."

"And don't think the media won't latch onto that? It's my shovel sticking out of his neck."

"Maybe you should wipe off your prints and stuff. You didn't get any DNA on him, did you?"

She stretched the front of her shirt out and started dabbing at the shovel's handle. "DNA? Like what?"

"You know, hair, blood, semen? Nothing like that?"

"No." She was furiously buffing the handle of the shovel with the front of her tank top, being careful not to get too close to the end that was stuck in the dead guy. Strangely, Tuck found the process slightly erotic.

"I think you got the fingerprints, but I'm a little concerned about there where your name is spelled out in Magic Marker on the handle. That might give things away."

"People never return garden tools if you don't mark them," Lena said. Then she began to cry again. "Oh my God, I've killed him."

Tuck went to her side and put his arm around her shoulders. "Hey, hey, hey, it's not so bad. At least you don't have kids you have to explain this to."

"What am I going to do? My life is over."

"Don't talk like that," Tuck said, trying to sound cheerful. "Look, you've got a perfectly good shovel here, and this hole is nearly finished. What say we shove Santa in, clean up the area a little, and I take you to dinner." He grinned.

She looked up at him.

"Who *are* you?"

"Just a nice guy trying to help out a lady in distress."

"And you want to take me out to dinner?" She seemed to be slipping into shock.

"Not this minute. Once we get this all under control."

"I just killed a man," she said.

"Yeah, but not on purpose, right?"

"A man I used to love is dead."

"Damn shame, too," Tuck said. "You like Italian?"

She stepped away from him and looked him up and down, paying special attention to the right shoulder of his bomber jacket, where the brown leather had been scraped so many times it looked like suede. "What happened to your jacket?"

"My fruit bat likes to climb on me."

"Your fruit bat?"

"Look, you can't get through life without accumulating a little baggage, right?" Tuck nodded toward the deceased to make his point. "I'll explain over dinner."

Lena nodded slowly. "We'll have to hide his truck."

"Of course."

"Okay, then," Lena said. "Would you mind pulling the shovel—uh, I can't believe this is happening."

"I got it," Tuck said, jumping into the hole and dislodging the spade from Saint Nick's neck. "Call it an early Christmas present."

Tuck took off his jacket and began digging in the hard ground. He felt light, a little giddy, thrilled that he wasn't going to have to spend Christmas alone with the bat again.

Chapter 4

HAVE YOURSELF A NASTY
LITTLE CHRISTMAS

Josh wiped the tears off his face, took a deep breath, and headed up the walk to his house. He was still shaking from having seen Santa take a shovel in the throat, but now it occurred to him that it might not be enough to get him out of trouble. The first thing his mom would say was, *Well, what were you doing out so late anyway?* And dumb Brian, who was not Josh's real dad but Mom's dumb boyfriend, would say, "Yeah, Santa would probably still be alive if you hadn't stayed so long at Sam's house." So, there on the front step, he decided to go with total hysteria. He started breathing hard, pumping up some tears, got a good whimpering sob going, then opened the door with a dieseling back sniffle. He fell onto the welcome mat and let loose with a full fire-truck-siren wail. And nothing happened. No one said a word. No one came running.

So Josh crawled into the living room, trailing a nice fiber-optic string of drool from his lower lip to the carpet as he chanted a mucusy "Momma," knowing that it would completely disarm her temper and get her all fired up to protect him from dumb Brian, for whom he had no magic manipulation chant. But nobody called him, nobody came running, dumb Brian was not sprawled across the couch like the great sleepy slug that he was.

Josh wound it down. "Mom?" Just the hint of a sob there, ready to go full bore again when she answered. He went into the kitchen, where the memo light was blinking on Mom's machine. Josh wiped his nose on his sleeve and hit the button.

"Hi, Joshy," his mom said, her cheerful overtired voice. "Brian and I had to go out to eat with some buyers. There's a Stouffer's mac and cheese in the freezer. We should be home before eight. Do your homework. Call my cell if you get scared."

Josh couldn't believe the luck. He checked the clock on the microwave. Only seven-thirty. Excellent! Latch-keyed loose like a magic elf. Yes! Dumb Brian had come through with a business dinner. He grabbed the Stouffer's out of the freezer, popped it—box and all—into the microwave, and hit the preset time. You didn't really have to peel the plastic back like they said. If you just nuke it in the box, the cardboard will keep it from exploding all over the microwave when the plastic goes. Josh didn't know why they didn't just put that in the instructions. He went back into the living room, turned on the TV, and plopped down on the floor in front of it to wait for the microwave to beep.

Maybe he should call Sam, he thought. Tell him about Santa. But Sam didn't believe in Santa. He said that Santa was just something the goys made up to make them feel better about not having a menorah. That was crap, of course. Goys (a Jewish word for girls and boys, Sam had explained) didn't want a menorah. They wanted toys. Sam was just saying that because he was mad because instead of Christmas they had snipped the tip of his penis off and said mazel tov.

"Wow, sucks to be you," said Josh.

"We're the Chosen," said Sam.

"Not for kickball."

"Shut up."

"No, you shut up."

"No, you shut up."

Sam was Josh's best friend and they understood each other, but would Sam know what to do about a murder? Especially a murder of an important person? You were supposed to go to an adult in these situations, Josh was pretty sure of it. Fire, an injured friend, a bad touch, you were supposed to tell an adult, a parent, a teacher, or a policeman, and no one would be mad at you. (But if you found your mom's boyfriend lighting a giant chili-dog-and-beer fart in the garage workshop, the police absolutely did not want to know about it. Josh had learned that lesson the hard way.)

A commercial came on, and Josh's mac and cheese was still surfing the microwaves, so he debated calling 911 or praying, and decided to go with the prayer. Like calling 911, you weren't supposed to pray for just anything. For instance, God did not care whether or not you got your bandicoot through the fire level on PlayStation, and if you asked for help there, there was a good chance that he would ignore you when you really needed help, like for a spelling test or if your mom got cancer. Josh reckoned it was sort of like cell-phone minutes, but this seemed like a real emergency.

"Our Heavenly Father," Josh began. You never used God's first name—that was like a commandment or something. "This is Josh Barker, six-seventy-one Worchester Street, Pine Cove, California nine-three-seven-five-four. I saw Santa tonight, which was great, and thank you for that, but then, right after I saw him, he got killed with a shovel, and so, I'm afraid that there's not going to be any Christmas and I've been good, which I'm sure you'll see if you check Santa's list, so if you don't mind, could you please make Santa come back to life and make everything okay for Christmas?" No, no, no, that sounded really selfish. Quickly he added: "And a Happy Hanukkah to you and all the Jewish people like Sam and his family. Mazel tov." There. Perfect. He felt a lot better.

The microwave beeped and Josh ran to the kitchen, right into the legs of a really tall man in a long black coat who was standing by the counter. Josh screamed and the man took him by the arms, picked him up, and looked him over like he was a gemstone or a really tasty dessert. Josh kicked and squirmed, but the blond man held him fast.

"You're a child," said the blond man.

Josh stopped kicking for a second and looked into the impossibly blue eyes of the stranger, who was now studying him in much the same way a bear might examine a portable television while wondering how to get all those tasty little people out of it.

"Well, duh," said Josh.

The Christmas tree took a wide left onto Cypress Street. Finding that somewhat suspicious, Constable Theophilus Crowe pulled in behind it as he dug the little blue light out of the glove compartment of his Volvo and stuck it on the roof. Theo was relatively sure that there was a vehicle under the Christmas tree somewhere, but all he could see right now were the taillights shining through the branches in the back. As he followed the tree up Cypress, past the burger stand and Brine's Bait, Tackle, and Fine Wines, a pinecone the size of a Nerf football broke loose and rolled off to the side of the street, bouncing and thumping into one of the gas pumps.

Theo hit the siren one time, just a chirp, thinking he'd better stop this before someone got hurt. There was no way that the driver under the Christmas tree could see the road clearly. The tree was driving trunk first, so the widest, thickest branches were covering the front of the vehicle. The tree's tires chirped with a downshift. It killed the lights and screeched around the corner on Worchester Street, leaving a trail of rolling pinecones and pine-fresh exhaust.

Under normal circumstances, if a suspect tried to elude Theo, he would have called it into the county sheriff's immediately, hoping a deputy in the area might provide backup, but he'd be damned if he was going to call in that he was in hot pursuit of a fugitive Christmas tree. Theo turned the siren onto full shriek and took off up the hill after the fleeing conifer, thinking for the fiftieth time that day that life had seemed a lot easier when he'd smoked pot.

"Boy, you don't see that every day," said Tucker Case, who was sitting at a window table at H.P.'s Café, waiting for Lena to come back from freshening up in the restroom. H.P.'s—a mix of pseudo Tudor and Country Kitchen Cute—was Pine Cove's most popular restaurant, and tonight it was completely packed.

The waitress, a pretty redhead in her forties, glanced up from the tray of drinks she was delivering and said, "Yeah, Theo hardly ever chases anyone."

"That Volvo was chasing a pine tree," Tuck said.

"Could be," said the waitress. "Theo used to do a lot of drugs."

"No, really—" Tuck tried to explain, but she had headed back to the kitchen. Lena was returning to the table. She was still in the black tank top under an open flannel shirt, but she had washed the streaks of mud from her face and her dark hair was brushed out around her shoulders. To Tuck she looked like the sexy but tough Indian guide chick in the movies, who always leads the group of nerdy businessmen into the wilderness where they are assaulted by vicious rednecks, bears gone mutant from exposure to phosphate laundry detergent, or ancient Indian spirits with a grudge.

"You look great," Tuck said. "Are you Native American?"

"What was the siren about?" Lena asked, sliding into the seat across from him.

"Nothing. A traffic thing."

"This is just so wrong." She looked around, as if everyone knew how wrong it was. "Wrong."

"No, it's good," Tuck said with a big smile, trying to make his blue eyes twinkle in the candlelight, but forgetting where exactly his twinkle muscles were located. "We'll have a nice meal, get to know each other a little."

She leaned over the table and whispered harshly, "There's a dead man out there. A man I used to be married to."

"Shh, shh, shh," Tuck shushed, gently placing a finger against her lip, trying to sound comforting and maybe a little European. "Now is not the time to talk of this, my sweet."

She grabbed his finger and bent it back. "I don't know what to do."

Tuck was twisted in his seat, leaning back to relieve the unnatural angle in which his finger was pointing. "Appetizer?" he suggested. "Salad?"

Lena let go of his finger and covered her face with her hands. "I can't do this."

"What? It's just dinner," said Tuck. "No pressure." He had never really dated much—gone on dates, that is. He'd met and seduced a lot of women, but it was never over a series of evenings with dinner and conversation—

usually just some drinks and vulgarity at an airport hotel lounge had done the trick. He felt it was time he
behaved like a grown-up—get to know a woman before he slept with her. His therapist had suggested it
right before she'd stopped treating him, right after he'd
hit on her. It wasn't going to be easy. In his experience
things went a lot better with women before they got
to know him, when they could still project hope and
potential on him.

"We just buried my ex-husband," Lena said.

"Sure, sure, but then we delivered Christmas trees to
the poor. A little perspective, huh? A lot of people have
buried their spouses."

"Not personally. With the shovel they killed him
with."

"You may want to keep it down a little." Tuck
checked the diners at the nearby tables to see if they
were listening, but they all seemed to be discussing the
pine tree that had just driven by. "Let's talk about something else. Interests? Hobbies? Movies?"

Lena tossed her head as if she didn't hear him right,
then stared as if to say, *Are you nuts?*

"Well, for instance," he pressed on, "I rented the
strangest movie last night. Did you know that *Babes in
Toyland* was a Christmas movie?"

"Of course, what did you think it was?"

"Well, I thought, well—now it's your turn. What's your favorite movie?"

Lena leaned close to Tuck and searched his eyes to see if he might be joking. Tuck batted his eyelashes, trying to look innocent.

"Who are you?" Lena finally asked.

"I told you."

"But, what's wrong with you? You shouldn't be so—so calm, while I'm a nervous wreck. Have you done this kind of thing before?"

"Sure. Are you kidding? I'm a pilot, I've eaten in restaurants all over the world."

"Not dinner, you idiot! I know you've had dinner before! What, are you retarded?"

"Okay, now everybody *is* looking. You can't just say 'retarded' in public like that—people take offense because, you know, many of them are. You're supposed to say 'developmentally disabled.'"

Lena stood up and threw her napkin on the table. "Tucker, thank you for helping me, but I can't do this. I'm going to go talk to the police."

She turned and stormed through the restaurant toward the door.

"We'll be back," Tuck called to the waitress. He nodded to the nearby tables. "Sorry. She's a little high-strung. She didn't mean to say 'retarded.'" Then he went after Lena, snatching his leather jacket off the back of his chair as he went.

He caught up with her as she was rounding the corner of the building into the parking lot. He caught her by the shoulder and spun her around, making sure that she saw that he was smiling when she completed the turn. Blinking Christmas lights played red and green highlights across her dark hair, making the scowl she was aiming at him seem festive.

"Leave me alone, Tucker. I'm going to the police. I'll just explain that it was just an accident."

"No. I won't let you. You can't."

"Why can't I?"

"Because I'm your alibi."

"If I turn myself in, I won't need an alibi."

"I know."

"Well?"

"I want to spend Christmas with you."

Lena softened, her eyes going wide, the swell of a tear watering up in one eye. "Really?"

"Really." Tuck was more than a little uncomfortable with his own honesty—he was standing like someone had just poured hot coffee in his lap and he was trying to keep the front of his pants from touching him.

Lena held out her arms and Tuck walked into them, guiding her hands inside his jacket and around his ribs. He rested his cheek against her hair and took a deep

breath, enjoying the smell of her shampoo and the residual pine scent picked up from handling the Christmas
trees. She didn't smell like a murderer—she smelled like
a woman.

"Okay," she whispered. "I don't know who you are,
Tucker Case, but I think I'd like to spend Christmas
with you, too."

She buried her face in his chest and held him until
there was a thump against his back, followed by a loud
scratching noise on his jacket. She pushed him back just
as the fruit bat peeked his little doggie face over the pilot's shoulder and barked. Lena leaped back and screamed
like a bunny in a blender.

"What in the hell is that?" she asked, backing across
the parking lot.

"Roberto," Tuck said. "I mentioned him before."

"This is too weird. Too weird." Lena began to chant
and pace in a circle, glancing up at Tuck and his bat
every couple of seconds. She paused. "He's wearing
sunglasses."

"Yeah, and don't think it's easy finding Ray·Bans in
a fruit-bat medium."

Meanwhile, up at the Santa Rosa Chapel, Constable
Theophilus Crowe had finally caught up to the fugitive
Christmas tree. He trained the headlights of the Volvo

on the suspect evergreen and stood behind the car door for cover. If he'd had a public-address system he would have used it to issue commands, but since the county had never given him one, he shouted.

"Get out of the vehicle, hands first, and turn and face me!"

If he'd had a weapon he would have drawn it, but he'd left his Glock on the top shelf of his closet next to Molly's old nicked-up broadsword. He realized that the car door was actually only providing cover to the lower third of his body, and he reached down and rolled up the window. Then, feeling awkward, he slammed the door and loped toward the Christmas tree.

"Goddammit, come out of the tree. Right now!"

He heard a car window whiz down and then a voice. "Oh my, Officer, you are so forceful." A familiar voice. Somewhere under there was a Honda CRV—and the woman he had married.

"Molly?" He should have known. Even when she stayed on her meds, as she had promised she would, she could still be "artistic." Her term.

The branches of the big pine tree shuffled and out stepped his wife, wearing a green Santa hat, jeans, red sneakers, and a jean jacket with studs down the sleeves. Her hair was tied back in a ponytail that trailed down her back. She might have been a biker elf. She rushed out of the branches as if she were ducking the blades of a helicopter, then ran to his side.

"Look at this magnificent son of a bitch!" She gestured to the tree, put her arm around his waist, pulled him close, humped his leg a little. "Isn't it great?"

"It certainly is—uh, large. How'd you get it on the car?"

"Took some time. I hoisted it up on some ropes, then drove under it. Do you think there'll be a flat spot where it dragged on the road?"

Theo looked the tree up and down, back and forth, watched the car exhaust boiling out of the branches. He wasn't sure he wanted to know, but he had to ask. "You didn't buy this at the hardware store, did you?"

"No, there was a problem with that. But I saved a ton of money. Cut it myself. Completely totaled my broadsword, but look at this son of a bitch. Look at this glorious bastard!"

"You cut it down with your sword?" Theo wasn't so worried about what she had cut it down with, but from where she'd cut it. He had a secret in the forest near their cabin.

"Yeah. We don't have a chain saw that I don't know about, do we?"

"No." Actually they did, in the garage, hidden behind some paint cans. He'd hidden it when her "artistic" mo-

ments had been more frequent. "That's not the problem, sweetie. I think the problem is that it's too big."

"No," she said, walking the length of the tree now,
pausing to jump through the branches and turn off the
Honda's engine. "That's where you're wrong. Observe,
double doors into the chapel."

Theo observed. The chapel did, indeed, have double
doors. There was a single mercury lamp illuminating
the gravel parking lot, but he could clearly see the little
white chapel, the shadows of gravestones showing dimly
behind it—a graveyard where they'd been planting Pine
Covers for a hundred years.

"And the ceiling in the main room is thirty feet tall
at the peak. This tree is only twenty-nine feet tall. We
pull it through the doors backward and stand that baby
up. I'll need your help, but, you know, you don't mind."

"I don't?"

Molly pulled open her jean jacket and flashed Theo,
exposing his favorite breasts, right down to the shiny
scar that ran across the top of the right one, cocked up
like a curious purple eyebrow. It was like unexpectedly
running into two tender friends, both a little pale from
being out of the sun, a tad humbled by time, but with
alert pink noses upturned by the night chill. And as
quickly as they appeared, the jacket was pulled shut and
Theo felt like he'd been shut out in the cold.

"Okay, I don't mind," he said, trying to buy time for the blood to return to his brain. "How do you know the ceiling is thirty feet tall?"

"From our wedding pictures. I cut you out and used you to measure the whole building. It was just under five Theos tall."

"You cut up our wedding pictures?"

"Not the good ones. Come on, help me get the tree off the car." She turned quickly and her jacket fanned out behind her.

"Molly, I wish you wouldn't go out like that."

"You mean like this?" She turned, lapels in hand.

And there they were again, his pink-nosed friends.

"Let's get the tree set up and then do it in the grave-yard, okay?" She jumped a little for emphasis and Theo nodded, following the recoil. He suspected that he was being manipulated, enslaved by his own sexual weakness, but he couldn't quite figure out why that was a bad thing. After all, he was among friends.

"Sweetheart, I'm a peace officer, I can't—"

"Come on, it will be *nasty*." She said *nasty* like it meant delicious, which is what she meant.

"Molly, after five years together, I'm not sure we're supposed to be nasty." But even as he said it, Theo was moving toward the big evergreen, looking for the ropes that secured it to the Honda.

Over in the graveyard, the dead, who had been listening all along, began to murmur anxiously about the new Christmas tree and the impending sex show.

They'd heard it all, the dead: crying children, wailing widows, confessions, condemnations, questions that they could never answer; Halloween dares, raving drunks—invoking the ghosts or just apologizing for drawing breath; would-be witches, chanting at indifferent spirits, tourists rubbing the old tombstones with paper and charcoal like curious dogs scratching at the grave to get in. Funerals, confirmations, communions, weddings, square dances, heart attacks, junior-high hand jobs, wakes gone awry, vandalism, Handel's *Messiah,* a birth, a murder, eighty-three Passion plays, eighty-five Christmas pageants, a dozen brides barking over tombstones like taffeta sea lions as the best man gave it to them dog style, and now and again, couples who needed something dark and smelling of damp earth to give their sex life a jolt: the dead had heard it.

"Oh yeah, oh yeah, oh yeah!" Molly cried from her seat astraddle the town constable, who was squirming on an uncomfortable bed of plastic roses a few feet above a dead schoolteacher.

"They always think they're the first ones. Ooooo, let's do

it in the graveyard," said Bess Leander, whose husband had served her foxglove tea with her last breakfast.

"I know, there are three used condoms on my grave from this week alone," said Arthur Tannbeau, citrus farmer, deceased five years.

"How can you tell?"

They heard everything, but their vision was limited.

"The smell."

"That's disgusting," said Esther, the schoolteacher.

It's hard to shock the dead. Esther was feigning disgust.

"What's all the racket? I was sleeping." Malcolm Cowley, antique book dealer, myocardial infarction over Dickens.

"Theo Crowe, the constable, and his crazy wife doing it on Esther's grave," said Arthur. *"I'll bet she's off her meds."*

"Five years they've been married and they're still at this kind of thing?" Since her death, Bess had taken a strong antirelationship stance.

"Postmarital sex is so pedestrian." Malcolm again, ever bored with provincial, small-town death.

"Some postmortem sex, that's what I could use," said the late Marty in the Morning, KGOB radio's top DJ with a bullet—a pioneer carjack victim back when hair bands ruled the airwaves. *"A rave in the grave, if you get my meaning."*

"Listen to her. I'd like to slip the bone to her," said Jimmy Antalvo, who'd kissed a pole on his Kawasaki to remain ever nineteen.

"Which one?" Marty cackled.

"The new Christmas tree sounds lovely," said Esther. *"I do hope they sing 'Good King Wenceslas' this year."*

"If they do," spouted the moldy book dealer, *"you'll find me justly spinning in my grave."*

"You wish," said Jimmy Antalvo. *"Hell, I wish."*

The dead did not spin in their graves, they did not move—nor could they speak, except to one another, voices without air. What they did was sleep, awakening to listen, to chat a bit, then, eventually, to never wake again. Sometimes it took twenty years, sometimes as long as forty before they took the big sleep, but no one could remember hearing a voice from longer ago than that.

Six feet above them, Molly punctuated her last few convulsive climactic bucks with, "I—AM—SO—GOING—TO—WASH—YOUR—VOLVO—WHEN—WE—GET—HOME! YES! YES! YES!"

Then she sighed and fell forward to nuzzle Theo's chest as she caught her breath.

"I don't know what that means," Theo said.

"It means I'm going to wash your car for you."

"Oh, it's not a euphemism, like, *wash the old Volvo.* Wink, wink, nudge, nudge?"

"Nope. It's your reward."

Now that they were finished, Theo was having a hard time ignoring the plastic flowers that were impressed in his bare backside. "I thought this was my reward." He gestured to her bare thighs on either side of him, the divots her knees had made in the dirt, her hair played out across his chest.

Molly pushed up and looked down at him. "No, this was your reward for helping me with the Christmas tree. Washing your car is your reward for this."

"Oh," Theo said. "I love you."

"Oh, I think I'm going to be sick," said a newly dead voice from across the woods.

"Who's the new guy?" asked Marty in the Morning.

The radio on Theo's belt, which was down around his knees, crackled. "Pine Cove Constable, come in. Theo?"

Theo did an awkward sit-up and grabbed the radio. "Go ahead, Dispatch."

"Theo, we have a two-oh-seven-A at six-seven-one Worchester Street. The victim is alone and the suspect may still be in the area. I've dispatched two units, but they're twenty minutes out."

"I can be there in five minutes," Theo said.

"Suspect is a white male, over six feet, long blond hair, wearing a long black raincoat or overcoat."

"Roger, Dispatch. I'm on my way." Theo was trying to pull his pants up with one hand while working the radio with the other.

Molly was on her feet already, naked from the waist down, holding her jeans and sneakers rolled up under her left arm. She extended a hand to help Theo up.

"What's a two-oh-seven?"

"Not sure," said Theo, letting her lever him to his feet. "Either an attempted kidnapping or a possum with a handgun."

"You have plastic flowers stuck to your butt."

"Probably the former, she didn't say anything about shots fired."

"No, leave them. They're cute."

Chapter 5

THE SEASON FOR MAKING
NEW FRIENDS

Theo was doing fifty up Worchester Street when the blond man stepped from behind a tree into the street. The Volvo had just lurched over a patched strip in the asphalt, so the grille was pointed up and caught the blond man about hip-high, tossing him into the air ahead of the car. Theo stood on the brake, but even as the antilocks throbbed, the blond man hit the tarmac and the Volvo rolled over him, making sickening crunching and thumping noises as body parts rico-cheted into wheel wells.

Theo checked the rearview as the car stopped and saw the blond man flopping to a stop in the red wash of the brake lights. Theo pulled the radio off his belt as he leaped from the car, and stood ready to call for help when the figure lying in the road started to get up.

Theo let the radio fall to his side. "Hey, buddy, just stay right there. Just stay calm. Help is on the way." He started loping toward the injured man, then pulled up.

The blond guy was on his hands and knees now; Theo could also see that his head was twisted the wrong way and the long blond hair was cascading back to the ground. There was a crackling noise as the guy's head turned around to face the ground. He stood up. He was wearing a long black coat with a rain flap. This was "the suspect."

Theo started backing away. "You just stay right there. Help is on the way." Even as he said it, Theo didn't think this guy was interested in any help.

The foot that faced backward came around to the front with another series of sickening crackles. The blond man looked up at Theo for the first time.

"Ouch," he said.

"I'm guessing that smarted," Theo said. At least his eyes weren't glowing red or anything. Theo backed into the open door of the Volvo. "You might want to lie down and wait for the ambulance." For the second time in as many hours, he wished he had remembered to bring his gun along.

The blond man held an arm out toward Theo, then

noticed that the thumb on the outstretched hand was on the wrong side. He grabbed it with his other hand and snapped it back into place. "I'll be okay," the blond man said, monotone.

"You know, if that coat dry-cleans itself while I'm watching, I'll nominate you for governor my own self," Theo said, trying to buy time while he thought of what he was going to say to the dispatcher when he keyed the button on the radio.

The blond man was now coming steadily toward him—the first few steps limping badly, but the limp getting better as he got closer. "Stop right there," Theo said. "You are under arrest for a two-oh-seven-A."

"What's that?" asked the blond man, now only a few feet from the Volvo.

Theo was relatively sure now that a 207A was not a possum with a handgun, but he wasn't sure what it was, so he said, "Freakin' out a little kid in his own home. Now stop right there or I will blow your fucking brains out." Theo pointed the radio, antenna first, at the blond guy.

And the blond guy stopped, only steps away. Theo could see the deep gouges cut in the man's cheeks from contact with the road. There was no blood.

"You're taller than I am," said the blond man.

Theo guessed the blond man to be about six-two,

maybe three. "Hands on the roof of the car," he said, training the antenna of the radio between the impossibly blue eyes.

"I don't like that," said the blond man.

Theo crouched quickly, making himself appear shorter than the blond man by a couple of inches.

"Thanks."

"Hands on the car."

"Where's the church?"

"I'm not kidding, put your hands on the roof of the car and spread 'em." Theo's voice broke like he was hitting second puberty.

"No." The blond man snatched the radio out of Theo's hand and crushed it into shards. "Where's the church? I need to get to the church."

Theo dove into the car, scooted across the seat, and came out on the other side. When he looked back over the roof of the car the blond man was just standing there, looking at him like a parakeet might look at himself in the mirror.

"What!?" Theo screamed.

"The church?"

"Up the street you'll come to some woods. Go through them about a hundred yards."

"Thank you," said the blond man. He walked off.

Theo jumped back into the Volvo, threw it into

drive. If he had to run over the guy again, so be it. But when he looked up from the dash, no one was there. It suddenly occurred to him that Molly might still be at the old chapel.

Her house smelled of eucalyptus and sandalwood and had a woodstove with a glass window that warmed the room with orange light. The bat was locked outside for the night.

"You're a cop?" Lena said, moving away from Tucker Case on the couch. She'd gotten past the bat. He'd explained the bat, sort of. He'd been married to a woman from a Pacific island and had gotten the bat in a custody battle. Things like that happened. She'd gotten the house they were sitting in, in her divorce from Dale, and it still had a black marble Jacuzzi tub with bronze Greek erotic figures inset in a border around the edge. The jetsam of divorce can be embarrassing, so you couldn't fault someone a bathtub or fruit bat rescued out of love's shipwreck, but he might have mentioned he was a cop before he suggested burying her ex and going to dinner.

"No, no, not a real cop. I'm here working for the DEA." Tuck moved closer to her on the couch.

"So you're a drug cop?" He didn't look like a cop. A golf pro, maybe, that blond hair and the lines around the eyes from too much sun, but not a cop. A TV cop, maybe—the vain, bad cop, who has something going on with the female district attorney.

"No, I'm a pilot. They subcontract independent helicopter pilots to fly agents into pot-growing areas like Big Sur so they can spot patches hidden in the forest with infrared. I'm just working for them here for a couple of months."

"And after a couple of months?" Lena couldn't believe she was worried about commitment from this guy.

"I'll try to get another job."

"So you'll go away."

"Not necessarily. I could stay."

Lena moved back toward him on the couch and examined his face for the hint of a smirk. The problem was, since she'd met him, he'd always worn the hint of a smirk. It was his best feature. "Why would you stay?" she said. "You don't even know me."

"Well, it might not be about you." He smiled.

She smiled back. It was about her. "It is about me."

"Yeah."

He was leaning over and there was going to be a kiss and that would be okay, she thought, if the night hadn't been so horrible. It would be okay if they hadn't shared so much history in so short a time. It would be okay if, if . . .

He kissed her.

Okay, she was wrong. It was okay. She put her arms around him and kissed him back.

Ten minutes later she was down to just her sweater and panties, she had driven Tucker Case deeply enough into the corner of the couch that his ears were baffled with cushions, and he couldn't hear her when she pushed back from him and said, "This doesn't mean that we're going to bed together."

"Me, too," said Tuck, pulling her closer.

She pushed back again. "You can't just assume that this is going to happen."

"I think I have one in my wallet," he said, trying to lift her sweater over her head.

"I don't do this sort of thing," she said, wrestling with his belt buckle.

"I had a test for my pilot physical a month ago," he said as he liberated her breasts from their combed cotton yoke of oppression. "Clean as a whistle."

"You're not listening to me!"

"You look beautiful in this light."

"Does doing this so soon after, you know—does doing this make me evil?"

"Sure, you can call it a weasel if you want to."

And so, with that tender honesty, that frank connection, the coconspirators chased away each other's loneliness, the smell of grave-digging sweat rising romantic in the room as they fell in love. A little.

Despite Theo's concern, Molly wasn't at the old chapel, she was getting a visit from an old friend. Not a friend, exactly, but a voice from the past.

"Well, that was just nuts," he said. *"You can't feel good about that."*

"Shut up," said Molly, "I'm trying to drive."

According to the *DSM-IV,* the *Diagnostic and Statistical Manual of Mental Disorders,* you had to have at least two of a number of symptoms in order to be considered as having a psychotic episode, or, as Molly liked to think of it, an "artistic" moment. But there was an exception, a single symptom that could put you in the batshit column, and that was "a voice or voices commenting on the activities of daily life." Molly called it "the Narrator," and she hadn't heard from him in over five years—not since she'd gone and stayed on her medication as she had promised Theo. That had been the agreement, if she stayed on her meds, Theo would stay off of his—well, more specifically, Theo would not have anything to do with his drug of choice, marijuana. He'd had quite a habit, going back twenty years before they'd met.

Molly had stuck to the agreement with Theo; she'd even gotten decertified by the state and gone off financial aid. A resurgence in royalties from her old movies had helped with the expenses, but lately she'd started falling short.

"*It's called an enabler,*" said the Narrator. "*The Drug Fiend and the Warrior Babe Enabler, that's you two.*"

"Shut up, he's not a drug fiend," she said, "and I'm not the Warrior Babe."

"*You did him right there in the graveyard,*" said the Narrator. "*That is not the behavior of a sane woman, that is the behavior of Kendra, Warrior Babe of the Outland.*"

Molly cringed at the mention of her signature character. On occasion, the Warrior Babe persona had leaked off the big screen and into her own reality. "I was trying to keep him from noticing that I might not be a hundred percent."

" '*Might not be a hundred percent*'? You were driving a Christmas tree the size of a Winnebago down the street. You're way off a hundred percent, darlin'. *"

"What do you know? I'm fine."

"*You're talking to me, aren't you?*"

"Well . . ."

"*I think I've made my point.*"

She'd forgotten how smug he could be.

Okay, maybe she was having a few more artistic moments than usual, but she hadn't had a break with reality. And it was for a good cause. She'd taken the money she'd saved on her meds to pay for a Christmas present for

Theo. It was on layaway down at the glass blower's gallery: a handblown dichromatic glass bong in the Tiffany style. Six hundred bucks, but Theo would so love it. He'd destroyed his collection of bongs and water pipes right after they'd met, a symbol of his break with his pot habit, but she knew he missed it.

"Yeah," said the Narrator. *"He'll need that bong when he finds out he's coming home to the Warrior Babe."*

"Shut up. Theo and I just had an adventurous romantic moment. I am not having a break."

She pulled into Brine's Bait, Tackle, and Fine Wines to pick up a six-pack of the dark bitter beer Theo liked and some milk for the morning. The little store was a miracle of eclectic supply, one of the few places on the planet where you could buy a fine Sonoma Merlot, a wedge of ripened French Brie, a can of 10W-30, and a carton of night crawlers. Robert and Jenny Masterson had owned the little shop since before Molly had come to town. She could see Robert by himself behind the counter, tall with salt-and-pepper hair, looking a little hangdog as he read a science magazine and sipped a diet Pepsi. Molly liked Robert. He'd always been kind to her, even when she was considered the village's resident crazy lady.

"Hey, Robert," she said as she came through the door. The place smelled of egg rolls. They sold them out of the back, where they had a pressure fryer. She breezed past the counter toward the beer cooler.

"Hey, Molly." Robert looked up, a little startled. "Uh, Molly, you okay?"

Crap, she thought. Had she forgotten to brush the pine needles out of her hair? She probably looked a mess. She said, "Yeah, I'm fine. Theo and I were just putting up the Christmas tree at the Santa Rosa Chapel. You and Jenny are coming to Lonesome Christmas, aren't you?"

"Of course," Robert said, his voice still a little strained. He seemed to be making an effort not to look at her. "Uh, Molly, we kind of have a policy here." He tapped the sign by the counter. NO SHIRT, NO SHOES, NO SERVICE.

Molly looked down. "Oh my gosh, I forgot."

"It's okay."

"I left my sneakers in the car. I'll just run out and put them on."

"That would be great, Molly. Thanks."

"No problem."

"I know it's not on the sign, Molly, but while you're out there, you might want to put some pants on, too. It's sort of implied."

"Sure thing," she said, breezing by the counter and out the door, feeling now that, yes, it seemed a little cooler out than when she'd left the house. And there were her jeans and panties on the passenger seat next to her sneakers.

"I told you," said the Narrator.

Chapter 6

BE OF GOOD CHEER;
THEY MIGHT HAVE PUT A TREE
UP YOUR BUM

The Archangel Raziel found, after some consideration, that he did not care for being run over by a Swedish automobile. As far as things "dirtside" went, he liked Snickers bars, barbecued pork ribs, and pinochle; he also enjoyed *Spider-Man, Days of Our Lives,* and *Star Wars* (although the concept of fictional film eluded the angel and he thought they were all documentaries); and you just couldn't beat raining fire on the Egyptians or smiting the bejeezus out of some Philistines with lightning bolts (Raziel was good with weather), but overall, he could do without missions to Earth, humans and their machines in general, and (now) Volvo station wagons in particular. His broken bones had knit nicely and the deep gouges in his skin were filling in even as he came upon the chapel, but all things considered, he could go a very long time not being run over by a Volvo again and feel just dandy about it.

He brushed at the all-weather radial tire print that ran up the front of his black duster and across his angelic face. Licking his lips, he tasted vulcanized rubber, thinking that it wouldn't be bad with hot sauce or perhaps chocolate sprinkles. (There is little variety of flavors in heaven, and an abundance of bland white cake has been served to the heavenly host over the eons, so Raziel had fallen in the habit of tasting things while dirtside, just for the contrast. Once, in the third century B.C., he had consumed the better part of a bucket of camel urine before his friend the Archangel Zoe slapped it out of his hand and informed him that it was, despite the piquant bouquet, nasty.)

This wasn't his first Nativity mission. No, in fact, he had been given the assignment of the very first Nativity mission, and due to having stopped on the way to play some pinochle, he'd shown up ten years late, announcing to the prepubescent Son himself that he "would find the babe wrapped in swaddling clothes, lying in a manger." Embarrassing? Well, yes. And now, some two thousand years later, he was on another Nativity mission, and he was sure now that he'd found the child, that this one was going to go much more smoothly (for one thing, there were no shepherds to frighten—he'd felt bad about that back then). No, come Christmas Eve the mission would be accomplished, he'd grab a plate of ribs and head back to heaven lickety-split.

But first he needed to find the site for the miracle.

There were two sheriff's cruisers and an ambulance outside the Barker house when Theo arrived.

"Crowe, where the hell have you been?" the sheriff's deputy was yelling before Theo was even out of the Volvo. The deputy was the second-shift commander; Joe Metz was his name. He had a linebacker frame that he augmented with weight lifting and marathon beer drinking. Theo had encountered him a dozen times in as many years. Their relationship had gone from a mild disregard to an open disrespect—which was pretty much Theo's relationship with everyone in the San Junipero County Sheriff's Department.

"I saw the suspect and made pursuit. I lost him in the woods about a mile east of here." Theo decided he wasn't going to mention what he'd actually seen. His credibility was thin enough with the sheriff's department.

"Why didn't you call it in? We should have units all over the area."

"I did. You do."

"I didn't hear the call go in."

"I called it in on my cell. My radio's broken."

"Why don't I know about it?"

Theo raised his eyebrows as if to say, *Perhaps because you're a big no-necked dumb-ass.* At least that's what he hoped the gesture said.

Metz looked at the radio on his belt, then turned to disguise his action as he turned a switch. Immediately the voice of the dispatcher came on, calling out for the shift commander. Metz keyed the mike clipped to the epaulet of his uniform shirt and identified himself.

Theo stood by, trying not to smile as the dispatcher reported the entire situation again. Theo wasn't worried about the two units that were headed to the woods up by the chapel. He was sure they weren't going to find anyone. Whoever the guy in black was, he had a way of disappearing, and Theo didn't even want to think of the means by which he did it. Theo had gone back to the chapel, where he'd caught a glimpse of the blond man moving through the woods before he was gone again. Theo had called home to make sure that Molly was okay. She was.

"Can I talk to the kid?" Theo asked.

"When the EMTs are done looking at him," Metz said. "The mother's on the way. She was out to dinner with the boyfriend in San Junipero. Kid seems okay, just real shaken up, some bruises on his arms where the suspect picked him up, but no other injuries I could see. Kid couldn't say what the guy wanted. There's no property missing."

"You get a description?"

"The kid keeps giving us names of characters from video games for comparison. What do we know from 'Mung-fu, the Vanquished'? You get a good look at him?"

"Yeah," Theo said, forcing a lump out of his throat, "I'd say Mung-fu is pretty accurate."

"Don't fuck with me, Crowe."

"Caucasian, long blond hair, blue eyes, clean-shaven, six foot two, one-eighty, wearing a black duster that goes to the ground. I didn't see his shoes. Dispatch has it all." Theo kept thinking of the deep gouges in the blond guy's cheeks. He had started to think of him as the "ghost-bot." Video games—right.

Metz nodded. "Dispatch says he's on foot. How'd you lose him?"

"The woods are thick up there."

Metz was looking at Theo's belt. "Where's your weapon, Crowe?"

"I left it in the car. Didn't want to scare the kid."

Without a word, Metz stepped over to Theo's Volvo and opened the passenger-side door. "Where?"

"Pardon?"

"Where in your *unlocked* car is your weapon?"

Theo felt the last of his energy flow out of him. He just wasn't good at confrontation. "It's at my house."

Metz smiled now like the bartender had just announced pitchers all around, on the house. "You know, you might be the perfect guy to go after this suspect, Theo."

Theo hated it when the sheriffs called him by his first name. "Why's that, Joseph?"

"The kid said he thought the guy might be retarded."

"I don't get it," Theo said, trying not to grin.

Metz walked away shaking his head. He climbed into his cruiser, then as he was backing past Theo, the passenger window whirred down. "Write up a report, Crowe. And we need to get a description of this guy to the local schools."

"It's Christmas break."

"Dammit, Crowe, they'll be going back to school sometime, won't they?"

"So you don't think your guys will catch him, then?"

Without another word Metz whirred up the window and whipped the cruiser out of the driveway as if he'd just received an urgent call.

Theo smiled as he walked up to the house. Despite the excitement and terror and outright weirdness of the evening, he suddenly felt good. Molly was safe, the kid was safe, the Christmas tree was up at the chapel, and there was just no rush that compared to safely and suc-cessfully fucking with a pompous cop. He paused on the top step and considered for a moment that perhaps, after fifteen years in law enforcement himself, he really should have matured past that particular pleasure.

Nah.

"Did you ever shoot anybody?" asked Joshua Barker. He was sitting on a bar stool at the kitchen counter. A man in a gray uniform was fussing medical over him.

"No, I'm an EMT," said the EMT. He ripped the blood-pressure cuff off Josh's arm. "We help people, we don't shoot them."

"Did you ever put that blood-pressure thing around someone's neck and pump it till their eyes bugged out?"

The EMT looked at Theophilus Crowe, who had just entered the Barkers' kitchen. Theo frowned appro-priately. Josh turned his attention to the lanky consta-ble, noting that he had a badge clipped to his belt but no gun.

"You ever shoot anybody?"

"Sure," Theo said.

Josh was impressed. He'd seen Theo around town, and his mom always said hi to him, but he never thought he actually did anything. Not anything cool, anyway. "None of these guys ever shot anyone." Josh gestured to the two deputies and the two EMTs stationed around the small kitchen, giving them a look that said *the wussies!* with the full disdain his soft seven-year-old features could muster.

"You kill the guy?" he asked Theo.

"Yep."

Josh didn't really know where to go now. If he stopped asking questions, he knew that Theo would start asking questions, just like the sheriffs had, and he didn't want to answer any more questions. The blond man had told him not to tell anyone. The sheriff said that the blond man couldn't hurt him, but the sheriff didn't know what Josh knew.

"Your mom is on the way, Josh," Theo said. "She'll be here in a few minutes."

"I know. I talked to her."

To the EMTs and deputies, Theo said, "Guys, can I talk to Josh alone a minute?"

"We're done here," the lead medic said, leaving immediately.

Both the deputies were young and eager to be asked to do something, even if it was to leave the room. "We'll be outside writing this up," said the last one out. "Sergeant Metz told us to stay until the mother got home."

"Thanks, guys," Theo said, surprised at their congeniality. They must not have been on the department long enough to learn to look down on him for being a town constable, an archaic and redundant job, if you asked most area cops.

Once they were gone he turned to Josh. "So tell me about the man who was here."

"I told those other police."

"I know. But you need to tell me. What happened. Even the weird stuff you didn't tell them."

Josh didn't like the way Theo seemed to be ready to believe anything. He wasn't being too nice, or talking baby talk like the others.

"There wasn't any weird stuff. I told them." Josh nodded as he spoke, hoping he'd look more convincing. "None of that bad touch stuff. I know about that. None of that."

"I don't mean that kind of stuff, Josh. I mean weird stuff you didn't tell them because it's unbelievable."

Josh really didn't know what to say now. He considered crying, did a test sniffle just to see if he could get things flowing. Theo reached out and took his chin, lifted it so Josh had to look him in the eye. Why did adults do that? Now he'd ask something that would be really hard to lie about.

"What was he doing here, Josh?"

Josh shook his head, mostly to get out of Theo's grip, to get away from that adult lie-detector look. "I don't know. He just came in and grabbed me and then he left."

"Why did he leave?"

"I don't know, I don't know. I'm just a kid. Because he's crazy or something. Or maybe he's retarded. That's how he talks."

"I know," Theo said.

"You do?" He did?

Theo leaned in close. "I saw him, Josh. I talked to him. I know he wasn't like a normal guy."

Josh felt like he'd just taken his first deep breath since he left Sam's house. He didn't like keeping secrets—sneaking home and lying about it would have been enough, but witnessing the murder of Santa, and then that strange blond guy showing up. But if Theo already knew about the blond guy . . . "So, so, you saw him glow?"

"Glow? Shit!" Theo stood up and spun around as if he'd been hit in the forehead with a paintball. "He glowed, too? Shit!" The tall man was moving like a grasshopper locked in a running microwave. Not that Josh would know what that was like, because that would be a cruel thing to do and he would never do something like that, but, you know, someone told him about it once.

"So he glowed?" Theo asked, like he was trying to get this straight.

"No, I didn't mean that." Josh needed to back out of this. Theo was trippin'. He'd had enough of adults trippin' for one night. Soon his mom would come home to find a bunch of cops in her house and the trip to beat all trips would start. "I mean he was really mad. You know, like glowing mad."

"That's not what you meant."

"It isn't?"

"He really glowed, didn't he?"

"Well, not constantly. Like, for a little while. Then he just stared at me."

"Why did he leave, Josh?"

"He said he had what he needed now."

"What was that? What did he take?"

"I don't know." Josh was beginning to worry about the constable. He looked like he might hurl any second. "You're sure you want to go with the glowing thing, Constable Crowe? I could be wrong. I'm a kid. We make notoriously unreliable witnesses."

"Where'd you hear that?"

"*CSI.*"

"Those guys know everything."

"They have the coolest stuff."

"Yeah," said Theo wistfully.

"You don't get to use cool cop stuff like that, huh?"

"Nope." Theo was sounding really sad now.

"But you shot a guy, right?" Josh said cheerfully, trying to raise Theo's spirits.

"I was lying. I'm sorry, Josh. I'd better go. Your mom will be home soon. You just tell her everything. She'll look out for you. The deputies will stay with you until she gets here. See ya, kiddo." Theo ruffled his hair and started out of the kitchen.

Josh didn't want to tell her. And he didn't want Theo to go. "There's something else."

Theo turned and looked back at him. "Okay, Josh, I'll stick around—"

"Someone killed Santa Claus tonight," Josh blurted out.

"Childhood ends too soon, doesn't it, son?" Theo said, putting his hand on Josh's shoulder.

If Josh had had a gun, he'd have shot him, but being an unarmed kid, he decided that of all of these adults, the goofy constable might just be the one who would believe what he had seen happen to Santa.

The two deputies had come into the house with Josh's mother, Emily Barker. Theo waited until she had hugged most of the breath out of her son, then reassured her that everything was okay and made a quick escape. As he came down the porch steps, he saw something yellow shining by the front tire of his Volvo. He looked back to make sure that neither of the deputies was looking out, then he crouched before the front tire and reached up into the wheel well and pulled out a hank of yellow hair that had caught in the black vinyl dent molding. He quickly shoved it into his shirt pocket and climbed into the car, feeling the hair throbbing against his chest like a living thing.

The Warrior Babe of the Outland admitted that she was powerless without her medication and that her life had become unmanageable. Molly checked off the step in Theo's little blue Narcotics Anonymous book.

"Powerless," she muttered to herself, remembering the time when mutants had chained her to a rock in the den of the behemo-badger in *Outland Steel: Kendra's Revenge.* If not for the intervention of Selkirk, the rogue sand pirate, her entrails would even now be curing on the salt stalagmites of the badger's cave.

"That would sting, huh?" said the Narrator.

"Shut up, that didn't really happen." *Did it?* She re-membered it like it did.

The Narrator was a problem. *The* problem, really. If it had just been a little erratic behavior, she might have been able to wing it until the first of the month and go back on her meds without Theo noticing, but when the

Narrator showed up, she knew she needed help. She turned to the Narcotics Anonymous book that had been Theo's constant companion when he was battling his pot habit. He talked about working the steps all the time, and how he couldn't have done it without them. She needed to do something to reinforce the rapidly blurring line between Molly Michon, party planner, cookie baker, the retired actress, and Kendra, mutant slayer, head breaker, the warrior temptress.

" 'Step two,' " she read. " 'Come to believe that a power greater than ourselves can restore us to sanity.' " She thought for a moment and looked out the front window of the cabin for the lights from Theo's car. She really hoped she could get through all twelve steps before he got home.

"Nigoth the Worm God shall be my higher power," she declared, snatching her broken broadsword from the coffee table and waving it in defiance at the Sony Wega TV that mocked her darkly from the corner. "In Nigoth's name shall I sally forth, and woe unto any mutant or sand pirate that crosses my path, for his life shall be sacrificed and his bloody balls shall decorate the totem tree of my lodge."

"And the wicked shall cower before the grandeur of your dirt-striped and well-shaped thighs," said the Narrator, with robust enthusiasm.

"Goes without saying," Molly said. "Okay, step

three. 'Turn your life over to God as you understand Him.' "

"Nigoth requires a sacrifice," cried the Narrator. *"A limb! Cut it from your body and impale it still twitching upon the worm god's fiery purple horn."*

Molly shook her head to rattle the Narrator around a little. "Dude," she said. Molly seldom "duded" anyone. Theo had picked up the word on his patrol of Pine Cove's skateboard park and now used it generally to express incredulity at the audacity of someone's statement or behavior—the correct inflection on the word would convey *Doood, please, you've got to be joking or hallucinating, or both, to even suggest such a thing.* (Lately Theo had been doing some testing on "Yo, dat's wack, yo." But Molly had forbade its use outside of the house, for, as she pointed out, there is little more off-putting than the sound of hip-hop vernacular coming out of the mouth of a white, fortysomething, goony bird of a man. "Albatross of a man, yo," Theo had corrected.)

Thusly duded, the Narrator bid devotion down. *"A finger, then! The severed finger of a Warrior Babe—"*

"Not a chance," Molly said.

"A lock of hair! Nigoth requires—"

"I was thinking I'd light a candle to symbolize that I'm turning myself over to my higher power." And to illustrate her sincerity, she took a disposable lighter off the coffee table and lit one of the scented candles she kept on a tray at the table's center.

"A snotty Kleenex, then!" tried the Narrator.

But Molly had moved on to step four in the book. " 'Make a searching and fearless moral inventory of yourself.' I have no idea what that means."

"Well, I'll be fucked in the ear by a blind spider monkey if I get it," said the Narrator.

Molly decided not even to acknowledge the Narrator on that one. After all, if the steps worked like she hoped they would, the Narrator was not going to be around for much longer. She dug into the little blue book in search of clarification.

Upon further reading, it appeared that you were supposed to make a list of all the things wrong with your character.

"Put down that you're fucking nuts," said the Narrator.

"Got it," Molly said. Then she noticed that the book recommended making a list of resentments. She wasn't exactly sure what she was supposed to do with them, but in fifteen minutes she had filled three pages with all variety of resentments, including both parents, the IRS, algebra, premature ejaculators, good housekeepers, French automobiles, Italian luggage, lawyers, CD packaging, IQ tests, and the fucktard who wrote the "Caution, pastry may be hot when heated" warning on the Pop-Tarts box.

She paused for a breather and was reading ahead to step five when headlights swept across the yard and raked the front of the cabin. Theo was home.

"'Step five,'" Molly read. "'Confess to our higher power and another human being the exact nature of our wrongs.'"

As Theo came through the door, Molly, her broken broadsword in hand, spun from the cinnamon candle of Nigoth the Worm God and said, "I confess! I did not file taxes for the years ninety-five through two thousand, I have eaten the radioactive flesh of mutants, and I resent the hell out of you for not having to squat when you pee!"

"Hi, honey," Theo said.

"Shut up, grommet," said the Warrior Babe.

"So I guess I'm not going to get my Volvo washed?"

"Quiet! I'm confessing over here, ingrate."

"That's the spirit!" said the Narrator.

Chapter 7

MORNING IS BROKEN

It was Wednesday morning, three days before Christmas, when Lena Marquez awoke to find a strange man in her bed. The phone was ringing and the guy next to her made a moaning sound. He was partially covered by the sheets, but Lena was pretty sure that he was naked.

"Hello," she said into the phone. She lifted the sheet to look. Yep, he was naked.

"Lena, there's supposed to be a storm on Christmas Eve and we were going to have Mavis barbecue for Lonesome Christmas but she can't if it's raining and I yelled at Theo last night and went out and walked around in the dark for two hours and I think he thinks I'm crazy and you should probably know that Dale didn't come home last night and his new—uh, the other, uh—the woman he lives with called Theo in a panic and he—"

"Molly?"

"Yeah, hi, how you doing?"

Lena looked at the clock on the nightstand, then back at the naked man. "Molly, it's six-thirty."

"Thanks. It's sixty-seven degrees here. I can see the thermometer outside."

"What's wrong?"

"I just told you: storm coming. Theo doubts sanity. Dale missing."

Tucker Case rolled over, and despite being half asleep, he appeared to be ready for action.

"Well would you look at that," Lena thought to herself, then she realized she'd said it into the phone.

"What?" said Molly.

Tuck opened his eyes and smiled at her, then followed her gaze south. He pulled the sheet out of her hand and covered himself. "That's not for you. I just have to pee."

"Sorry," Lena said, pulling the sheet quickly over her head. It had been a long time since she'd had to worry about it, but she suddenly remembered a magazine article about not letting a man see you first thing in the morning unless he'd known you for at least three weeks.

"Who was that?" Molly said.

Lena made an eye tunnel in the sheet and looked out at Tucker Case, who was getting out of bed, totally unself-conscious, totally naked, his unit leading him into the bathroom, waving before him like a divining rod. She realized right then that she could always find new reasons to resent the male of the species—unself-consciousness was going on the list.

"No one," Lena said into the phone.

"Lena, you did not sleep with your ex again? Tell me you are not in bed with Dale."

"I'm not in bed with Dale." Then the whole night came rolling back on her and she thought she might throw up. Tucker Case had made her forget for a while. Okay, maybe she could count that as a positive toward men, but the anxiety was back. She'd killed Dale. She was going to jail. But she needed to pretend she didn't know anything.

"What did you say about Dale, Molly?"

"So who are you in bed with?"

"Dammit, Molly, what happened to Dale?" She hoped she sounded convincing.

"I don't know. His new girlfriend called and said he didn't come home after the Caribou Christmas party. I just thought you should know, you know, in case it turns out that something bad happened."

"I'm sure he's okay. He probably just met some tramp at the Head of the Slug and sold her on his workingman charm."

"Yuck," Molly said. "Oh, sorry. Look, Lena, they said on the news this morning that a big storm is coming in off the Pacific. We're going to have El Niño this year. We have to figure out something for the food for Lonesome Christmas—not to mention what to do if a lot of people show up. The chapel is awfully small."

Lena was still trying to figure out what to do about Dale. She wanted to tell Molly. If anybody would understand, it would be Molly. Lena had been around a couple of times when Molly had gone through her "breaks." She understood things getting out of control.

"Look, Molly, I need—"

"And I yelled at Theo last night, Lena. Really bad. He hasn't taken off like that in a long time. I may have fucked Christmas up."

"Don't be silly, Mol, you couldn't do that. Theo understands." Meaning, *He knows you're crazy and loves you anyway.*

Just then, Tucker Case came back into the room, retrieved his pants from the floor, and started pulling them on.

"I've got to go feed the bat," Tuck said. He pulled a banana partially out of his front pocket.

Lena threw the sheets off her head and tried to think of something to say.

Tuck grinned, pulling the banana all the way out. "Oh, you thought I was just glad to see you?"

"Uh—I—shit."

Tuck stepped over and kissed her eyebrow. "I *am* glad to see you," he said. "But I have to feed the bat, too. I'll be right back."

He walked out of the room, barefoot and shirtless. Okay, he probably would be back.

"Lena, who was that? Tell me?"

Lena realized that she was still holding the phone. "Look, Molly, I'll have to call you back, okay? We'll figure something out for Friday night."

"But, I have to make amends—"

"I'll call you." Lena hung up and crawled out of bed. If she was quick she could wash her face and get some mascara on before Tucker got back. She started zooming around the room, naked, until she felt someone watching her. There was a big bay window that looked out on a forest, and since her bedroom was on the second floor, it was like waking up in a tree house, but no one could possibly look in. She spun around and there, hanging from the gutter, was a giant fruit bat. And he was looking at her—no, not just looking at her, he was checking her out. She pulled the sheet off the bed and covered herself.

"Go eat your banana," she shouted at the bat.

Roberto licked his chops.

There had been a time, during his bong-rat years, when Theophilus Crowe would have stated, with little reservation, that he did not like surprises, that he preferred routine over variety, predictability over uncertainty, the known over the unknown. Then, a few years ago, while working on Pine Cove's last murder case, Theo had gotten to know and fallen in love with Molly Michon, the ex–scream queen of the B-movie silver screen, and everything changed. He had broken one of the cardinal rules—*Never go to bed with anyone crazier than yourself*—and he'd been loving life ever since.

They had their little agreement, if he stayed off his drug (pot) she'd stay on hers (antipsychotics), and consequently she'd have his unmuddled attention and he'd only get the most pleasant aspects of the Warrior Babe persona that Molly sometimes slipped into. He'd learned to delight in her company and the occasional weirdness that she brought into his life.

But last night had been too much for him. He'd come through the door wanting, nay, *needing* to share his bizarre story about the blond man, with the only person who actually might believe him and not berate him for being a stoner, and she had chosen that precise moment to lapse into hostile batshit mode. So, he'd fallen off the wagon, and by the time he returned to their cabin that night, he had smoked enough pot to put a Rastafarian choir in a coma.

That's not what the pot patch he'd been growing had been for. Not at all. Not like the old days, when he maintained a small victory garden for personal use. No, the little forest of seven-foot sticky bud platforms that graced the edge of their lot on the ranch was purely a commercial endeavor, albeit for the right reason. For love.

Over the years, even as the prospect of ever returning to the movies became more remote, Molly had continued to work out with her giant broadsword. Stripped to her underwear, or dressed in a sports bra and sweatpants, every day in the clearing in front of the cabin she'd declare *"en garde"* to an imaginary partner and proceed to spin, leap, thrust, parry, hack, and slash herself breathless. Beyond the fact that the ritual kept her incredibly fit, it made her happy, which, in turn, pleased Theo to no end. He'd even encouraged her to get involved in Japanese kendo, and to little surprise, she was excellent at it, consistently winning matches against opponents nearly twice her size.

And indirectly, all this had led to Theo's growing pot commercially for the first time in his life. He'd tried other means, but banks seemed more than a little reluctant to lend him nearly a half year's salary in order to purchase a samurai sword. Well, not samurai precisely, but a Japanese sword—an ancient Japanese sword, made by the master swordmaker Hisakuni of Yamashiro in the late thirteenth century. Sixty thousand folded layers of high carbon steel, perfectly balanced, and razor sharp even eight hundred years later. It was a *tashi,* a curved cavalry sword, longer and heavier than the traditional *katana*s used later by samurais in ground combat. Molly would appreciate the weight during her workouts, as its heft was closer to that of the theatrical broadsword she'd brought with her as a legacy of her failed movie career. She would also appreciate that it was real, and Theo hoped that she'd see that it was his way of saying that he loved all the parts of her, even the Warrior Babe (he just liked rubbing up against some parts more than others). The *tashi* was now wrapped in velvet and hiding at the back of the top shelf of Theo's closet, where he used to keep his bong collection.

The money? Well, an old friend of Theo's from the stoner days, a Big Sur grower now turned wholesaler, had been happy to advance Theo the money against his crop. It was supposed to have been a purely commercial venture: get in, get out, and nobody gets hurt. But now Theo was showing up stoned for work for the first time in years, and following a bad night, he could just sense that this wasn't going to be a good day.

Then the call came in from Dale Pearson's girlfriend/wife/whatever, and the descent into hell day started.

Theo drowned his eyes in Visine and stopped at Brine's Bait, Tackle, and Fine Wines for a large coffee before he headed over to Lena Marquez's house in search of her ex-husband. While it was clear from the incident at the Thrifty-Mart on Monday, and a dozen earlier incidents, that their dislike for each other bordered on hatred, it hadn't stopped them from hooking up from time to time for some familiar post-divorce sex. Theo wouldn't have even known about it, except Molly was good friends with Lena and women talked about that sort of thing.

Lena lived in a nice two-story Craftsman-style house on a half acre of pine forest that butted up to one of Pine Cove's many ranches. It was more house than she would have been able to afford working as a property manager, but then, she had put up with Dale Pearson for five years of marriage, and for five years since, so it was the least she deserved, Theo thought. He liked the sound of his hiking boots on the porch as he walked to the front door, and he thought that he and Molly should build a porch on their little cabin. He thought they could maybe get a wind chime, and a swing, have a little heater so they could sit outside on cold evenings. Then he realized, as he felt that vibration of footsteps coming to the door, that he was totally and completely baked. That they would know he was baked. That no amount of Visine or coffee was going to cover the fact that he was baked. Twenty years of functioning stoned was not going to serve him now—he'd lost his edge, he was no longer in the game, the eye of the tiger was bloodshot.

"Hi, Theo," Lena said, opening the door. She wore a man's oversize sweatshirt and red socks. Her long black hair, which normally flowed down her back like liquid satin, was all knotted up at the back of her head, and there was a big tangle sticking out by one ear. Sex hair.

Theo shuffled on the porch like a kid getting ready to ask the girl next door for a first date. "I'm sorry to bother you so early, but I wondered if you've seen Dale. Since Monday, I mean."

She seemed to fade away from the door, like she was ready to faint. Theo was sure it was because she knew he was high. "No, Theo. Why?"

"Well, uh, Betsy called, and said that Dale didn't come home last night." Betsy was Dale's new wife/girlfriend/whatever. She was a waitress down at H.P.'s Café and over the years had become notorious for having affairs with a lot of married guys. "I was just, uh . . ." Why wouldn't she interrupt him? He didn't want to say that he knew that she and Dale got together for spite sex occasionally. He wasn't supposed to know. ". . . so, uh, I was just wondering."

"Hi, who's this?" said a blond guy who had appeared shirtless behind Lena in the doorway.

"Oh, thank God," Theo said, taking a deep breath. "I'm Theo Crowe, I'm the town constable." He looked at Lena for an introduction.

"This is Tucker—uh, Tuck."

She had no idea what this guy's last name was.

"Tucker Case," said Tucker Case, stepping around Lena and offering his hand to shake. "I should have introduced myself to you sooner, I guess, since we're in the same business."

"What business is that?" Theo never thought of himself as being a businessman, but he guessed that he was now.

"I'm flying helicopter for the DEA," said Tucker Case. "You know, infrared, finding growers and stuff."

Clear! His heart has stopped! Code blue! Five hundred milligrams of epinephrine, direct shot to the pericardium, stat! He's flatlining, people. Clear!

"Nice to meet you," Theo said, hoping his heart failure wasn't showing. "Well, sorry to bother you. I'll just be on my way." He let go of Tuck's hand and started walking away, thinking: *Don't walk stoned, don't walk stoned—for the love of God, how did I do this all of those years?*

"Uh, Constable," Tuck said. "Why was it that you stopped by? Ouch!"

Theo turned. Lena had just punched the pilot in the arm, evidently pretty hard—he was massaging it.

"Uh, nothing. Just a fellow didn't go home last night, and I thought Lena might have an idea where he went." Theo was trying to back away from the house, but then stopped, remembering that he might trip on the porch steps. How would he explain that to the DEA?

"Last night? That's not even a missing person for, what, twenty-four, forty-eight hours? Ouch! Dammit, that's not necessary." Tucker Case rubbed his shoulder where Lena had punched him again.

Theo thought that she might have violence issues with men.

Lena looked at Theo and grinned, as if she was embarrassed about the punch. "Theo, Molly called me this morning and told me about Dale. I told her I hadn't seen him. Didn't she tell you?"

"Sure. Sure, she told me. I just, you know, I thought you might have some ideas. I mean, your friend is right, Dale's not really missing, officially, for another twelve hours or so, but, you know, it's a small town, and I, you know, have a job and stuff."

"Thanks, Theo," Lena said, waving to him even though he was only a few feet away and wasn't moving away from the house. The pilot was waving, too, smiling. Theo didn't like being around new lovers who had just gotten laid, especially when things weren't going that well in his own love life. They seemed smug, even if they weren't trying to be.

He spotted something dark swinging from the ceiling of the porch, right where the wind chime would have been on his and Molly's porch, if he hadn't just sacrificed their security by relapsing into dope-fiendism. It couldn't be what it looked like.

"So, that's a, uh, that looks like——"

"A bat," said Lena.

Holy fuck, Theo thought, *that thing is huge.* "A bat," he said. "Sure. Of course."

"Fruit bat," Tucker Case clarified. "From Micronesia."

"Oh, right," Theo said. Micronesia was not a real place. The blond guy was fucking with him. "Well, I'll see you guys."

"See you at Lonesome Christmas on Friday," Lena said. "Say hi to Molly."

" 'Kay," Theo said, climbing into the Volvo.

He closed the car door. They went inside. He let his head hit the steering wheel.

They know, he thought.

"He knows," Lena said, her back against the front door.

"He doesn't know."

"He's smarter than he looks. He knows."

"He doesn't know. And he didn't look dumb, he looked kind of stoned."

"No, he wasn't stoned, that was suspicion."

"Don't you think if he was suspicious he might have asked where you were last night?"

"Well, he could see that, with you walking out there with your shirt off, and me looking so, you know—so—"

"Satisfied?"

"No, I was going to say 'disheveled.'" She punched his arm. "Jeez, get over yourself."

"Ouch. That is completely out of line."

"I'm in trouble here," Lena said. "You can at least be supportive."

"Supportive? I helped you hide the body. In some countries that implies commitment."

She wound up to punch him, then caught herself, but left her fist there in the air, just in case. "You really don't think he was suspicious?"

"He didn't even ask why you have a giant fruit bat hanging out on your porch. He's oblivious. Just going through the motions."

"Why *do* I have a giant fruit bat hanging from the porch?"

"Comes with the package." He grinned and walked away.

Now she felt stupid, standing there, her fist in the air.

She felt unenlightened, dense, silly, unevolved, all the things she thought only other people were. She followed him into the bedroom, where he was putting on his shirt.

"I'm sorry I hit you."

He rubbed his bruised shoulder. "You have tendencies. Should I hide your shovel?"

"That's a horrible thing to say." She almost punched him, but instead, trying to be more evolved, and less threatening, she put her arms around him. "It was an accident."

"Release me. I have to go spot bad guys with my helicopter," he said, patting her on the bottom.

"You're taking the bat with you, right?"

"You don't want to hang out with him?"

"No offense, but he's a little creepy."

"You have no idea," said Tuck.

Chapter 8

HOLIDAY HEARTBREAK

Christmas Amnesty. You can fall out of contact with a friend, fail to return calls, ignore e-mails, avoid eye contact at the Thrifty-Mart, forget birthdays, anniversaries, and reunions, and if you show up at their house during the holidays (with a gift) they are socially bound to forgive you—act like nothing happened. Decorum dictates that the friendship move forward from that point, without guilt or recrimination. If you started a chess game ten years ago in October, you need only remember whose move it is—or why you sold the chessboard and bought an Xbox in the interim. (Look, Christmas Amnesty is a wonderful thing, but it's not a dimensional shift. The laws of time and space continue to apply, even

if you *have been* avoiding your friends. But don't try using the expansion of the universe as an excuse—like
you kept meaning to stop by, but their house kept getting farther away. That crap won't wash. Just say, "Sorry
I haven't called. Merry Christmas." Then show the present. Christmas Amnesty protocol dictates that your
friend say, "That's okay," and let you in without further
comment. This is the way it has always been done.)

"Where the fuck have you been?" said Gabe Fenton
when he opened the door and saw his old friend
Theophilus Crowe standing there, holding a present.
Gabe, forty-five, short and wiry, unshaven and slightly
balding, was wearing khakis that looked like he'd slept
in them for a week.

"Merry Christmas, Gabe," said Theo, holding out
the present, a big red bow on it—sort of waving the box
back and forth as if to say, *Hey, I have a present here, you're
not supposed to sandbag me for not calling for three years.*

"Yeah, nice," said Gabe. "But you might have called."

"Sorry. I meant to, but you were involved with Val, I
didn't want to interrupt."

"She dumped me, you know?" Gabe had been seeing
Valerie Riordan, the town's only psychiatrist, for several
years now. Not for the last month, however.

"Yeah, I heard about that." Theo had heard that Val
wanted someone who was a little more involved with
human culture than Gabe.

Gabe was a behavioral field biologist who studied wild rodents or marine mammals, depending on who was providing the funding. He lived at a small federally owned cottage by the lighthouse with his hundred-pound black Labrador retriever, Skinner.

"You heard? And you didn't call?"

It was nearly noon, and Theo's buzz had mostly worn off, but he was still thrown. Guys were not supposed to lament the lack of support from a friend, unless it was backup in a bar fight or help in moving heavy stuff. This was not normal behavior. Maybe Gabe really did need to spend more time around human beings.

"Look, Gabe, I brought you a present," Theo said. "Look at how glad Skinner is to see me."

Skinner was, in fact, glad to see Theo. He was crowding Gabe in the doorway, his beefy tail beating against the open door like a Snausage war drum. He associated Theo with hamburgers and pizza, and had once thought of him as the emergency backup Food Guy (Gabe being the primary Food Guy).

"Well, I suppose you should come in," said Gabe. The biologist stepped away from the door and allowed Theo to enter. Skinner said hi by shoving his nose into Theo's crotch.

"I'm working in here, so things are a little messy."

A little messy? An understatement on a par with calling the Bataan Death March a nature hike—it looked like someone had loaded all of Gabe's belongings into a cannon and fired them into the room through the wall. Dirty laundry and dishes covered every surface except for Gabe's worktable, which, except for the rats, was immaculate.

"Nice rats," Theo said. "What are you doing with them?"

"I'm studying them."

Gabe sat down in front of a series of five-gallon aquariums arranged around a center tank in a star pattern and linked by Habitrail tubes, with gates for routing rats from one chamber to another. Each of the rats had a silver disk about the size of a quarter glued to its back.

Theo watched as Gabe opened a gate and one of the rats rushed to the center tank and immediately tried to mount its occupant. Gabe picked up a small remote control and hit the button. The attacking rat nearly did a backflip trying to retreat.

"Ha! That'll teach 'im," Gabe shouted. "The female in the center cage is in estrus."

The rat backed away tentatively and did some sniffing, then attempted to mount the female again. Gabe hit the button. The male was jolted off of her.

"Ha! Now do you get it?!" Gabe said maniacally. He looked up from the cages to Theo. "There are electrodes on their testes. The silver disks are batteries and remote receivers. Every time he gets sexually aroused, I'm hitting his little nuts with fifty volts."

The rat made another attempt and again Gabe hit the button. The rat spazzed its way to the corner of the cage.

"You stupid shit!" Gabe shouted. "You think they'd learn. I'll hit each of them with the jolt a dozen times today, but when I open the cage tomorrow, they'll all run back in and try to mount her again. You see, you see how we are?"

"We?"

"Us. Males. See how we are. We know there's going to be nothing but pain, but we go back again and again."

Gabe had always been so steady, so calm, so professionally detached, scientifically obsessed, so dependably nerdy—Theo felt as if he were talking to a whole different person, like someone had scrubbed off all the intellect and had exposed the nerves. "Uh, Gabe, I'm not sure that we should equate ourselves with rodents. I mean—"

"Oh, sure. That's what you say now. But you'll call me and tell me I was right. Something will happen and you'll call. She'll stomp your heart and you'll finish the destruction she starts. Am I right? Am I right?"

"Uh, I—" Theo was thinking about the graveyard sex followed by the fight he'd had with Molly last night.

"So I'm going to change the association. Watch

this." Gabe stormed over to a bookshelf, threw aside a bunch of professional journals and notebooks until he found what he was looking for. "See. See her." Gabe held up a recent Victoria's Secret catalog. The model on the front was wearing garments spectacularly inadequate in concealing her appeal. She looked as if she just couldn't be happier about it. "Beautiful, right? Amazing, right? Hold that thought." Gabe reached into the pocket of his khakis and pulled out a stainless remote just like the one on the rat table. "Beautiful," he said, and he hit the button.

The biologist's back arched and he suddenly became six inches taller, all the muscles of his body seeming to flex at once. He convulsed twice, then fell to the floor, the crumpled catalog still in his hand.

Skinner lapsed into a barking fit. *Don't die, Food Guy, my bowl is on the porch and I can't open the door by myself,* he was saying. It was the same every time, he was always glad when the Food Guy wasn't actually dead, but the Food Guy's convulsions made him anxious.

Theo rushed to his friend's aid. Gabe's eyes were rolled back and he twitched a couple of times before he sucked in a deep breath and looked Theo in the eye. "See. You change the association. Won't be long and I'll have that reaction without the electrodes glued to my scrotum."

"Are you okay?"

"Oh yeah. It will take hold, I know it. It hasn't worked with the rats yet, but I'm hoping it will before they all die."

"They're dying of this?"

"Well, it has to hurt or they'll never learn." Gabe held up his remote again and Theo snatched it out of his hand.

"Stop it!"

"I have another set of electrodes and receiver. You want to try it? I've been dying to try it out in the field. We could go to a titty bar."

Theo helped Gabe to his feet, then set him in a chair facing away from the rat table and pulled a chair around for himself.

"Gabe, you are out of control. I'm sorry I didn't call."

"I know you've been busy. It's okay."

Great, now he has the appropriate Christmas Amnesty reaction, Theo thought. "These rats, the electrodes, all of it, it's just wrong. You're just going to end up with either a bunch of paranoid misogynist males, or a pile of corpses."

"You make that sound like a bad thing."

"You got your heart broken. It will heal."

"She said I was dull."

"She should see this." Theo gestured around the room.

"She wasn't interested in my work."

"You guys had a good run. Five years. Maybe it was just time. You told me yourself that the human male was not evolved for monogamy."

"Yeah, but I had a girlfriend when I said that."

"So it's not true?"

"No, it's true, but it didn't bother me when I had a girlfriend. Now I know that I am biologically programmed to spread the seed of my loins far and wide, to as many females as possible, a series of torrid, meaningless matings, only to move on to the next fertile female. My genes are demanding that I pass them on, and I don't know where to start."

"You might want to shower before you start the seed spreading."

"You don't think I know that? That's why I was trying to reprogram my impulses. Tame the animus, as it were."

"Because you don't want to shower?"

"No, because I don't know how to talk to women. I could talk to Val."

"Val was a pro."

"She was not. She never turned a trick in her life."

"*Listener,* Gabe. She was a *pro listener*—a psychiatrist."

"Oh, right. Do you think I should start with a prostitute, or 'tutes?"

"For a broken heart? Yeah, I'm sure that will work just as well as the electrodes on your scrotum, but first I need you to do something for me." Theo thought maybe, just maybe, work—nonfreakish work—might bring his friend back from the brink. He reached into his shirt pocket and pulled out the hank of yellow hair he'd taken out of the Volvo's wheel well. "I need you to look at this and tell me about it."

Gabe took the hair and looked at it. "Is this crime stuff?"

"Sort of."

"Where did you get it? What do you need to know?"

"Tell me everything you can about it before I tell you anything, okay?"

"Well, it appears to be blond."

"Thanks, Gabe, I was thinking maybe you could look at it under the microscope or something."

"Doesn't the county have a crime lab for that?"

"Yeah, but I can't take it to them. There are circumstances."

"Like?"

"Like they will think I'm stoned or nuts or both. Look at the hair," Theo said. "You tell me. I'll tell you."

"Okay, but I don't have all that cool *CSI* stuff."

"Yeah, but the guys at the crime lab don't have batteries Super-Glued to their gonads. You've got them there."

Ten minutes later Gabe looked up from his microscope. "Well, it's not human," he said.

"Swell."

"In fact, it doesn't appear to be hair."

"So what is it?"

"Well, it seems to have a lot of the qualities of optic fiber."

"So it's man-made?"

"Not so fast. It has a root, and what appears to be a cuticle, but it doesn't look like keratin. I'd have to have it tested for proteins. If it's manufactured, there's no evidence of the process. It looks as if it was grown, not made. You know polar-bear hair has fiber-optic properties—channels light energy through to the black skin for heat."

"So it's polar-bear hair?"

"Not so fast."

"Gabe, goddammit, where in the hell did it come from?"

"You tell me."

"Just us, okay? This doesn't leave this cottage unless we get some confirmation, okay?"

"Of course. Are you okay, Theo?"

"Am I okay? You're asking me if I'm okay?"

"Everything all right with you and Molly? The job? You're not smoking dope again, are you?"

Theo hung his head. "You say you have another one of those electrodes?"

Gabe brightened. "You'll need to shave a spot. Can I open my present while you're in the bathroom? You can use my razor."

"No, go ahead and open your present. I have some stuff I need to tell you."

"Wow, a salad shooter. Thanks, Theo."

"He took the salad shooter," Molly said.

"Wow, was that important to him?" Lena asked.

"It was a wedding present."

"I know, I gave it to you. It was a wedding present to me and Dale, too."

"See, there was tradition." Molly was inconsolable. She drank off half of her diet Coke and slammed the plastic Budweiser cup down on the bar like a pirate cursing over a schooner of grog. "Bastard!"

It was Wednesday evening, and they were at the Head of the Slug saloon to coordinate the replanning of the food for the Christmas for the Lonesome party. Lena's first reaction to Molly's call to help was to beg off and stay at home, but even as she was creating an excuse, she realized that she'd only sit home obsessing alternately on getting caught for killing Dale and getting her heart broken by this strange, strange helicopter pilot. She decided that maybe meeting with Molly and Mavis down at the Slug wasn't such a bad idea. And she might be able to find out from Molly if Theo suspected her in Dale's disappearance. Yeah, fat chance, with Molly obsessing on Theo's—whatever it was that Theo was supposed to have done wrong. It sounded to Lena like he had just taken a salad shooter to work with him. You were supposed to empathize with your friend's problems, but they were, after all, your friend's problems, and Lena's friends, Molly in particular, could be a little wacky.

The bar was full of singles in their twenties and thirties and you could feel a desperate energy sparking around the dark room, like loneliness was the negative and sex was the positive and someone was brushing the wires together over an open bucket of gasoline. This was the fallout of the holiday heartbreak cycle that started with young men who, lacking any stronger motivation toward changing their lives, would break up with their current girlfriend in order to avoid having to buy her a Christmas present. The distraught women would sulk for a few days, eat ice cream, and avoid calling relatives, but then, as the idea of a solitary Christmas and New Year started to loom large, they swarmed into the Slug in search of a companion, virtually any companion, with whom they could pass the holidays. Full speed ahead and forget the presents. Pine Cove's male singles, to display their newfound freedom, would descend on the Slug, and avail themselves of the affections of dejected women in a game of small-town sexual musical chairs played hungrily to the tune of "Deck the Halls"—everyone hoping to have slipped drunkenly into someone more comfortable before the last fa was la-la-ed.

There might have been a bubble around Lena and Molly, however, for they were obviously not part of the game. While both were certainly more than attractive enough to garner attention from the younger men, they had about them a mystique of experience, of having been there and moved on, of unbullshitability. Essentially, they scared the hell out of all but the drunkest of the Slug's suitors, and the fact that they were drinking straight diet Coke scared the hell out of the drunks. Molly and Lena, despite their own personal distress, had slain their own holiday desperation dragons, which was how the Lonesome Christmas party had started in the first place. Now they were on to new, individual anxieties.

"Sloppy joes," said Mavis, a great cloud of low-tar smoke powering the announcement and washing over

Lena and Molly. It had been illegal to smoke in California bars for years, but Mavis ignored the law and the authorities (Theophilus Crowe) and smoked on. "Who doesn't like his meat sloppy on a bun?"

"Mavis, it's Christmas," Lena said. So far Mavis had only suggested soupy or saucy entrées—Lena suspected that Mavis had misplaced her dentures again and was therefore lobbying for a gummable feast.

"With pickles, then. Red sauce, green pickles, Christmas theme."

"I mean shouldn't we do something nice for Christmas? Not just sloppy joes?"

"At five bucks a head, I told her that barbecue was the only way to feed them." Mavis leaned in and looked at Molly, who was muttering malevolently into her ice cubes. "But everyone seems to think it's going to rain. Like it ever rains in December."

Molly looked up and growled a little, then looked at the television screen behind Mavis and pointed. The sound was muted, but there was a weather map of California. About eight hundred miles off the coast there was a great blob of color whirling in jump-frame satellite-photo motion, making it appear that a Technicolor amoeba was about to consume the Bay Area.

"Ain't nothin'," Mavis said. "They won't even give it a name. If that thing was crouched like that over

Bermuda, they'd have given it a name two days ago. Know why? 'Cause they don't come onshore here. That bitch will turn right a hundred miles off Anacapa Island and go down and dump all over the Yucatán. Meanwhile we won't be able to wash our cars because of the drought."

"The rain at least will stop any sand-pirate attacks," Molly said, crunching an ice cube.

"Huh?" said Lena.

"The hell did you say?" Mavis adjusted her hearing aid.

"Nothing," Molly said. "What do you guys think about lasagna? You know, some garlic bread, a little salad."

"Yeah, we can probably do it for five bucks a head if we don't use sauce or cheese," said Mavis.

"Lasagna just doesn't seem very Christmasy," said Lena.

"We could put it in Santa Claus pans," Molly suggested.

"No!" Lena snapped. "No Santas! We can do a snowman or something, but no friggin' Santas."

Mavis reached over and patted Lena's hand. "Santa played a little grab-ass with a lot of us when we were little, darlin'. Once your mustache starts growing you're supposed to let go of that shit."

"I am not growing a mustache."

"Do you wax? Because you can't see a thing," said Molly, being supportive.

"I do not have a mustache," said Lena.

"You think it's bad being a Mexican, Romanian women have to start shaving when they're twelve," Mavis said.

Lena took that opportunity to plant her elbows squarely on the bar and grip two great handfuls of her hair, which she began to pull, slowly and steadily, to make her point.

"What?" said Mavis.

"What?" said Molly.

And there was an awkward moment of silence among the three—only the muted jukebox thumping in the background and the low murmur of people lying to one another. They looked around to avoid talking, then turned to the front door as Vance McNally, Pine Cove's senior EMT, came through it and let loose a long, growling belch.

Vance was in his midfifties, and fancied himself a charmer and a hero, when, in fact, he was a bit of a dolt. He had been driving the ambulance for over twenty years now, and nothing gave him pleasure like being the bearer of bad news. It was the measure of his importance.

"You guys hear that the highway patrol found Dale Pearson's truck parked up in Big Sur by Lime Kiln

Rock? Looks like he was fishing and fell in. Yep, surf coming up from that storm, they'll never find him. Theo's up there now investigating."

Lena stumbled back to her bar stool and climbed up. She was sure everyone in the bar, all the locals anyway, were looking at her for a reaction. She let her long hair hang down by her face, hiding in it.

"So, lasagna it is," said Mavis.

"But no fucking Santa pans!" Lena snapped, not looking up.

Mavis pulled both of their plastic cups off the bar. "Normal circumstances, you'd be cut off, but as it is, I think you two really need to *start* drinking."

Chapter 9

THE LOCAL GUYS, THEY HAVE
THEIR MOMENTS

Thursday morning it became official: Dale Pearson, evil developer, was a missing person. Theo Crowe was going over the big red truck parked by the pounding Pacific at Lime Kiln Rock in the Big Sur wilderness area above Pine Cove. This was the area where half the world's car commercials were filmed—everything from Detroit minivans to German lux-o-cruisers was filmed snaking around the cliffs of Big Sur, as if all you needed to do was sign the lease papers and your life would be an open road of frothy waves beating on majestic seawalls, with nothing but leisure and prosperity ahead. Dale Pearson's big red truck did look carefree and prosperous, parked there by the sea, despite the crust of salt forming on the paint and the appearance that the owner had been washed away in the surf.

Theo wanted that to be the case. The highway patrol, who had found the truck, had reported it as an accident. There was a surf-casting rod there on the rocks, conveniently monogrammed with Dale's initials. And the Santa hat he'd been wearing was found washed up nearby, and therein lay the problem. Betsy Butler, Dale's squeeze, had said that Dale had gone out two nights ago to play Santa at the Caribou Lodge and had never come home. Who went fishing in the middle of the night while wearing a Santa hat? Granted, according to the other Caribou, Dale had done "some drinking," and he was a little wound up from his confrontation with his ex-wife the day before, but he hadn't lost his mind completely. Negotiating the cliffs by Lime Kiln Rock to get down to the water during the day was risky business; there's no way that Dale would have tried it in the middle of the night. (Theo had lost his footing and slid twenty feet before he caught himself, wrenching his back in the process. Sure he was a little stoned, but then, Dale would have been a little drunk.)

The highway patrolman, who had a crew cut and looked to be about twelve—an escapee from one of the hygiene films Theo had seen in sixth-grade health class, *Why Mary Won't Go in the Water*—had Theo sign off on his report, then climbed in his cruiser and headed up the coast into Monterey County. Theo went back and looked through the truck again.

All the things that should have been there—some tools, a black Mag flashlight, a couple of fast-food wrappers, another fishing rod, a tube of blueprints—were there. And all the things that shouldn't—bloody knives, shell casings, severed limbs, evidence of bleach from cleanup—were not. It was like the guy had just driven up here, climbed down the cliff, and washed away. But that just couldn't be the case. Dale could be mean-spirited, crude, and even violent, but he wasn't stupid. Unless he knew the exact topography of these cliffs, and had a good flashlight, he'd never have made it down in the dark. And his flashlight was still in the truck.

Theo wished that he had better training in crime-scene investigation. He'd learned most of what he knew from television, not at the academy where he'd spent a miserable eight weeks fifteen years ago when the corrupt sheriff who had found his personal pot patch had railroaded him into becoming Pine Cove's constable. Since the academy, almost every crime scene he'd encountered had been turned over to the county sheriff or highway patrol almost immediately.

He went over the truck cab again looking for something that might be a clue. The only thing remotely out of order was some dog hairs on the headrest. Theo couldn't remember if Dale had a dog.

He put the dog hairs in a sandwich bag and dialed Betsy Butler on his cell phone.

She didn't sound that broken up about Dale's disappearance. "No, Dale didn't like dogs. He didn't like cats either. He was kind of a cow man."

"He liked cows? Did you guys have a pet cow?" Could it be cow hair?

"No, he liked to eat them, Theo. Are you okay?"

"No, sorry, Betsy." He had been so sure that he didn't sound stoned.

"So, do I get the truck? I mean, are you going to bring it here?"

"I have no idea," said Theo. "They'll tow it to the impound yard. I don't know if they'll release it to you. I'd better go, Betsy." He snapped the phone shut. Maybe he was just tired. Molly had made him sleep on the couch last night—saying something about him having mutant tendencies. He hadn't even known that she liked the salad shooter. He was sure that she could tell that he'd been smoking pot.

He flipped the phone back open and called Gabe Fenton.

"Hey, Theo. I don't know what that stuff is you brought me, but it's not hair. It won't burn or melt, and it's damn hard to cut or break. Good thing it was torn out by the roots."

Theo cringed. He had almost forgotten about the

crazed blond guy he'd run over. He shuddered now, thinking about it. "Gabe, I have some more hair I'd like you to look at."

"Oh my God, Theo, did you run over someone else?"

"No, I didn't run over anybody. Jeez, Gabe."

"Okay. I'll be here all day. Actually, I'll be here all night, too. It's not like I have anywhere to go. Or anyone who cares whether I live or die. It's not like—"

"Okay. I'm coming over."

There were two men and three women, including Lena, in the offices of Properties in the Pines when Tucker Case came through the door. The women were immediately intrigued by him and the men immediately disliked him. It had always been that way with Tuck. Later, if they got to know him, the women would dismiss him and the men would still dislike him. Basically, he was a geek in a cool guy's body—one feature or the other worked against him.

It was an open stable of desks and Tuck went directly to Lena's desk at the back. As he went he smiled and nodded to the realtors, who smiled back weakly, trying not to sneer. They were beat from showing properties to Christmas vacation be-backs who wouldn't move here even if they could find employment in this toy town. They'd just failed to plan any vacation activities and so decided to take the kids out for a rousing round of jerk off the realtor. Or so went the party line at the MLS meetings.

Lena met Tuck's gaze and instinctively smiled, then frowned.

"What are you doing here?"

"Lunch? You. Me. Eating. Talking. I need to ask you something."

"I thought you were supposed to be flying."

Tuck hadn't seen Lena in her business clothes—a sensible skirt and blouse, just a little mascara and lipstick, her hair pinned up with lacquered chopsticks, a few strands escaping here and there to frame her face. He liked the look.

"I flew all morning. There's weather. The edge of a storm coming." He really wanted to pull the chopsticks out of her hair and throw her down there on the desk and tell her how he really felt, which was somewhat aroused. "We could get Chinese," he added.

Lena looked out the window. The sky was going dark gray over the shops across the street. "There's no Chinese place in Pine Cove. Besides, I'm really swamped here. I handle vacation rentals and it's Christmas Eve eve."

"We could go to your place for a quick lunch. You have no idea how quick I can be if I put my mind to it."

Lena looked past him to her coworkers, who, of course, were now staring. "Is that what you need to ask me?"

"Oh, no, no, of course not. I wouldn't—that would be, well, yes—but there's something else." Now Tuck was feeling the realtors watching him, listening to him. He leaned over Lena's desk so only she could hear. "You said this morning that that constable guy your friend is married to lives in a cabin at the edge of a ranch. It wouldn't be the big ranch north of town, would it?"

Lena was still looking past him. "Yes, the Beer-Bar Ranch, belongs to Jim Beer."

"And there's an old single-wide trailer next to the cabin?"

"Yes, that used to be Molly's, but now they live in the cabin. Why?"

Tuck stood back and grinned. "Then white roses it is," he said, a little too loudly for the benefit of the audience. "I just didn't know if they'd be appropriate for the holidays."

"Huh?" Lena said.

"See you tonight," Tuck said. He leaned over and kissed her on the cheek, then sauntered out of the office, smiling apologetically at the exhausted realtors as he went.

"Merry Christmas, you guys," he said, waving from the door.

The first thing that Theo noticed when he entered Gabe Fenton's cabin was the aquariums with the dead rats. The female was scampering around the center cage, sniffing and crapping and looking rat-happy, but the others, the males, lay on their backs, feet shot to the sky, like plastic soldiers in a death diorama.

"How did that happen?"

"They wouldn't learn. Once they associated the shock with sex, they started liking it."

Theo thought about his relationship with Molly over the last few days. He pictured himself in the dead-rat display. "So you just kept shocking them until they died?"

"I had to keep the parameters of the experiment constant."

Theo nodded gravely, as if he understood completely, which he didn't. Skinner came over and head-butted him in the thigh. Theo scratched his ears to comfort him.

Skinner was worried about the Food Guy, and he was hoping that maybe the Emergency Backup Food Guy might give him one of the tasty-smelling white squirrels in the cages on the table, now that it appeared that the

Food Guy was finished cooking them. This teasing was as bad as when that kid at the beach used to pretend to throw the ball, then not throw the ball. Then pretend to throw the ball, but not throw the ball. Skinner *had* to knock the kid down and sit on his face. Boy, had he been *bad-dogged* for that. Nothing hurt like being bad-dogged, but if the Food Guy kept teasing him with the white squirrels, Skinner knew he was going to have to knock him down and sit on his face, maybe even poop in his shoe. *Oh, I am a bad, bad dog.* No, wait, the Emergency Backup Food Guy was scratching his ears. Oh, that felt good. He was fine. Doggie Xanax. Never mind.

Theo handed Gabe the sandwich bag with the hairs in it.

"What's the oily substance in the bag?" Gabe said, examining the specimen.

"Potato-chip flotsam. The bag is from my lunch yesterday."

Gabe nodded, then looked at Theo the way the coroner always looks at the cop on TV—like: *You numb-skull, don't you know that you're contaminating evidence just by continuing to draw breath and I'd be a lot more comfortable with you if you'd stop?*

He took the bag over to the microscope on the counter, removed a couple of the hairs, and put them on a slide with a cover, then fitted it into the microscope.

"Please don't tell me it's polar bear," Theo said.

"No, but at least it's an animal. It seems to have a distinct sour-cream-and-onion signature." Gabe pulled back from the microscope and grinned at Theo. "Just fucking with you." He gave Theo a gentle punch to the arm and looked back into the microscope. "Wow, the medulla is absent and there's low birefringence."

"Wow," echoed Theo, trying but not really feeling the low-birefringence stoke that Gabe was.

"I have to check the hair database online, but I think it's from a bat."

"There's a database for that? What, Bat Hair Dot-Com?"

"That was supposed to be the whole purpose of the Internet, you know. To share scientific information."

"Not a Viagra- and porn-delivery system?" Theo said. Maybe Gabe was going to be okay after all.

Gabe moved to the computer at his desk and scrolled through screen after screen of microscope photos of mammal hair until he found one he liked, then went back to the microscope and checked it again.

"Wow, Theo, you've got yourself an endangered species here."

"No way."

"Where the hell did you get this? Micronesian giant fruit bat."

"Out of a Dodge pickup truck."

"Hmm, that's not listed as their habitat. It wasn't parked in Guam, was it?"

Theo fished his car keys out of his pocket. "Look, Gabe, I have to go. Meet at the Slug for a beer tonight, okay?"

"We can have beer now, if you want. I have some in the fridge."

"You need to get out. I need to get out. Okay?" Theo was backing out the door.

"Okay. I'll meet you at six. I have to go pick up some Super Glue solvent at the Thrifty-Mart."

"Bye." Theo jumped off the porch and loped to the Volvo.

Skinner barked at him in four-four time. *Hello? Tasty white squirrels? Still in the little box? Hello? You forgot?*

When Theo pulled up to Lena Marquez's house, there was a generic white economy rental car (*A Ford Mucus,* he thought) parked out front. He looked for the bat he'd seen hanging from the porch ceiling, but it wasn't there. He hadn't even filed the experience of running over the apparently indestructible blond guy, and now he was facing the possibility that he might actually be about to confront a murderer. Just in case, he'd stopped at home and gotten his gun off the shelf in the closet and his handcuffs off the bedpost where Molly had last imprisoned him when they had still been speaking. (She'd been in the yard out behind the cabin, working out with a bamboo *shinai* kendo sword she'd been using since breaking her broadsword—he'd snuck in and out without confrontation.) He unsnapped the Glock's nylon holster that was clipped to the back of his jeans and rang the doorbell.

The door opened. Theo screamed and drew his gun as he jumped back.

On the other side of the threshold, Tucker Case screamed and dove backward also, shielding his face with his hands. His bat made a little yelping sound.

"Hold it right there," Theo said. He could feel his pulse beating in his neck.

"I'm holding, I'm holding. Jesus, what the fuck is this about?"

"You have a bat on your head!"

"Yeah, and for that you're going to shoot me?"

The bat, his huge black wings wrapped around the pilot's head, gave the impression of a large leather cap with a Mohawk crest of fur that culminated in a big-eared little dog face that was now barking at Theo.

"Well, uh, no." Theo lowered the gun, feeling a little embarrassed now. He was still in his shooter's crouch, though, which now, with the gun lowered, made him look like he was posing as the world's skinniest sumo wrestler.

"Can I get up?" Tuck asked.

"Sure, I just wanted to talk to Lena."

Tucker Case was exasperated and his bat had fallen over one eye. "Well, she's at her office. Look, if you're going to get high, maybe you ought to leave the gun at home, huh?"

"What?" Theo had been careful to use some Visine, and it had been hours since he'd hit his Sneaky Pete pot pipe. He said, "I'm not high. I haven't gotten high in years."

"Yeah, right. Constable, maybe you'd better come in."

Theo stood and tried to shake off the appearance that he'd just had about five years of life scared out of him by a guy with a bat on his head. He followed Tucker Case into Lena's kitchen, where the pilot offered him a seat at the table.

"So, Constable, what can I do for you?"

Theo wasn't sure. He'd planned on talking to Lena, or at least the two of them together. "Well, as you probably know, we found Lena's ex-husband's truck up in Big Sur."

"Of course, I saw it."

"You saw it?"

"From the helicopter. Tucker Case, contract pilot for

the DEA, remember? You can check me out if you want to. Anyway, we've been patrolling that area."

"You have?" The bat was looking at Theo and Theo was having trouble following his own thoughts. The bat was wearing tiny sunglasses. Ray·Bans, Theo could see by the trademark in the corner of one lens. "I'm sorry, Mr., uh—Case, could you take the bat off your head. It's very distracting."

"Him."

"Pardon?"

"It's a him. Roberto. He no like the light."

"Pardon?"

"Friend of mine used to say that. Sorry." Tucker Case unwrapped the bat and put it on the floor, where it spidered away, walking on its wing tips into the living room.

"God, that's creepy," Theo said.

"Yeah, you know, kids. What are you gonna do?" Tuck dazzled a perfect grin. "So, you found this guy's truck? Not him, though?"

"No. It was made to look like he was washed into the ocean while fishing off the rocks."

"Made to look? So, you suspect foul play?" Tuck bounced his eyebrows.

Theo thought the pilot should be taking this more seriously. It was time to drop the bomb. "Yes. First, he never came home after the Caribou Christmas party Tuesday night, where he played the joke Santa. No one goes surf-fishing in the middle of the night, wearing a Santa suit. We found the Santa hat still in the truck, and I found hairs from a Micronesian fruit bat on the headrest."

"Well, that's a coincidence. Jeez, that's got to make you suspicious, doesn't it?" Tucker Case got up and went over to the counter. "Coffee? I just made it."

Theo stood up, too, just because he didn't want the suspect to get away, or maybe to show that he was taller, because it seemed like the only advantage he had over the pilot.

"Yes, it is suspicious. And I talked to a kid Tuesday night who said he saw a woman killing Santa Claus with a shovel. I didn't think anything of it then, but now I think the kid might have actually seen something."

Tucker Case was busying himself with getting cups out of the cupboard, milk out of the fridge. "So, you *did* tell the kid that there's no Santa, right?"

"No, I didn't."

Now Tucker Case turned, coffeepot in hand, and regarded Theo. "You know that there is no Santa, don't you, Constable?"

"This is not a joke," Theo said. He hated this—hated being the MAN. He was supposed to be the smart-ass in the face of authority figures.

"Cream?"

Theo sighed. "Sure. And sugar, please."

Tuck finished preparing the coffee, brought the cups to the table, and sat down.

"Look, I see where you're going with this, Theo. Can I call you Theo?"

Theo nodded.

"Thanks. Anyway, Lena was with me Tuesday night, all night."

"Really? I saw Lena on Monday. She didn't mention you. Where did you meet?"

"At the Thrifty-Mart. She was a Salvation Army Santa. I thought she was attractive, so I asked her out. We hit it off."

"You make it a habit of hitting on the Salvation Army Santas?"

"Lena said that you're married to a scream queen called Kendra, Warrior Babe of the Outland."

Theo nearly shot coffee out his nose. "That was a character she used to play."

"Yeah, Lena says sometimes that's not so clear to her. My point is: Love is where you find it."

Theo nodded. Yeah, that was true. Before he drifted into a wistful state of mind, Theo reminded himself that this guy was, in an offhand way, attacking the woman he loved. "Hey," Theo said.

"It's okay? Who am I to judge? I married an island girl who had never seen indoor plumbing until I brought her to the States. Didn't work out—"

"Fruit-bat hair in the truck," Theo interrupted.

"Yeah, I knew you'd come back to that. Well, who knows? Roberto goes out on his own from time to time. Maybe he met this Dale guy. Maybe they hit it off. You know, love is where you find it. I doubt it, though. I hear that this Dale guy was a real creep."

"Are you implying that your bat may have something to do with the disappearance of Dale Pearson?"

"No, you nitwit, I'm saying that my bat may have had something to do with bat hair, which, even you, with your Sherlock Holmes–like powers of observation, may have noticed he is all covered with."

"I can't believe you're a cop," Theo said, getting truly angry now.

"I'm not a cop. I just fly the helicopter for the DEA. They hire me by the season, and this is close to the harvest season in Big Sur and surrounding areas, so here I am, flying around looking in the forest for dark green patches while the agents in the back look at it through infrared and record everything on GPS so they can get specific warrants. And man, do they pay well. 'Vive la war on drugs,' I say. But no, I'm not a cop."

"I didn't think so."

"Funny thing is, I have learned to spot the right color of green from the sky, and usually the infrared confirms my suspicions. This morning I spotted about a thousand-square-foot patch of marijuana growing just north of the Beer–Bar Ranch. You know where that is?"

Theo felt a lump in his throat the size of one of Gabe's dead rats. "Yes."

"Man, that's a lot of pot, even by commercial growers' standards. Felony quantity. I turned the helicopter—steered away without calling it to the agent's attention, but weather permitting, we could go back. There's a storm coming in, you know? Roberto and I drove by there this afternoon just to make sure. I guess I can always show the agents tomorrow." Tucker Case put down his coffee, leaned on his elbows, and turned his head sideways like he was a cute kid in a cereal commercial who was reaching sugar nirvana.

"You're a very unlikable man, Mr. Case."

"Oh my God, you should have seen me before I had my epiphany. I used to really be an asshole. I'm actually very charming now. By the way, I saw your wife working out in the yard at your house—very nice. The whole sword thing is a little scary, but otherwise, very nice."

Theo got to his feet, feeling a little dizzy even as he stood, like he'd been hit with a sock full of sand. "I'd better be going."

Tucker Case put his hand on Theo's shoulder as he walked him to the door. "You probably don't believe this, Theo, but at another time, I'm sure we'd be friends. And you have to understand, I really, really want things to work out with Lena. It was like we met just at the precise moment, the exact second, that I got over my divorce and was ready to love again. And it's so nice to have someone to bone under the Christmas tree, don't you think? She's a great woman."

"I like Lena," Theo said. "But *you* are a psychopath."

"You think?" Tuck said. "I've really been trying to be more helpful."

Chapter 10

LOVE, KICKED TO THE CURB

"You did what?" Lena said, then adding, "And take that bat off your head, it's unnerving to have a hat looking at you like that."

"Like what?" Tuck said.

"Don't change the subject. You blackmailed Theo Crowe?" She was pacing her kitchen. Tuck sat at the counter, wearing a gold oxford-cloth shirt that complemented the bat on his head while accentuating the sea blue of his eyes. The bat, for once, wasn't wearing sunglasses.

"Not really. It was only sort of implied. He'd figured out that I'd been in your ex-husband's truck. He knew. Now he'll just forget it."

"He may not. He may have some integrity, unlike some people."

"Hey, hey, hey. Let's not point the finger here, my ex is still living well in the Caymans on money that I rightfully stole from an organ-smuggling doctor, while yours, need I remind you—"

"Dale's death was an accident. Everything since then, all this craziness, has been your doing. You come into my life at the worst possible moment, like you had a plan all along, and things have gone more and more out of control. Now you're blackmailing my friends. Tucker, are you insane?"

"Sure."

"Sure? Just like that? *Sure,* you're insane?"

"Sure, everyone is. If you think anyone is sane you just don't know enough about them. The key—and this is very relevant in our case—is to find someone whose insanity dovetails with your own. Like us." He flashed what Lena thought was supposed to be a charming grin, which was somewhat defused by his trying to untangle one of Roberto's wing claws from his hair.

Lena turned from him and leaned against the counter in front of the dishwasher, hoping to steel herself for what she had to do. Unfortunately Tuck had just run a load of dishes and the steam from the vent in front was streaming through her thin skirt and making her feel inappropriately moist for righteous indignation. She spun around with resolve and allowed the dishwasher to steam her backside as she made her pronouncement.

"Look, Tucker, you are a very attractive man . . ." She took a deep breath on the pause.

"No way. You're breaking up with me?"

"And I do like you, despite the situation—"

"Oh, right, you don't want to have anything to do with an attractive guy who you like, heaven forbid—"

"Would you shut up!"

The bat barked at her tone.

"You, too, fur face! Look, in another time and place, maybe. But you're too—I'm too—you just accept things too easily. I need—"

"Your anxiety?"

"Would you please let me finish?"

"Sure, go ahead." He nodded. The bat, now on his shoulder, nodded as well. Lena had to look away.

"And your bat is freaking me out."

"Yeah, well, you should have been around when he used to talk."

"Out! Tucker! I need you out of my life. I have too much to deal with—*you* are too much to deal with."

"But the sex, it was great, it was—"

"I understand if you want to go to the authorities— I may even go myself—but this just isn't right."

Tucker Case hung his head. Roberto the fruit bat hung his head. Tucker Case looked at the fruit bat, who, in turn, looked at Lena, as if to say, *Well, I hope you're happy, you broke his heart.*

"I'll get my stuff," Tuck said.

Lena was crying, and she didn't want to be crying, but she was. She watched Tuck pick up his things around the house and stuff them into a flight bag, wondering how he had spread so much crap around her house in only two days. Men, they were always marking territory.

He paused at the door and looked back. "I'm not going to go to the authorities. I'm just going to go."

Lena rubbed her forehead as if she had a headache but mainly to cover her tears. "Okay, then."

"I'm going, then . . ."

"Good-bye, Tucker."

"You won't have anyone to sex up under the Christmas tree . . ."

Lena looked up. "Jeez, Tuck."

"Okay. I'm going now." And he did.

Lena Marquez went into her bedroom to call her friend Molly. Maybe crying over the phone to a girlfriend would bring a sense of normalcy back into her life.

Sour Nerds? Cinnamon Geeks? Or Gummy Boogers? Sam Applebaum's mom was picking out a "nice" reasonably priced Cabernet, and Sam was allowed one item of candy from the rack at Brine's Bait, Tackle, and Fine Wines. Of course the Boogers would last the longest, but they were all mundane green-apple finish, while the Nerds proffered a fruity variety and an impudent little top note of tang. Cinnamon Geeks had a rich nose and a bit of a bite up front, but their tiny certified-public-accountant shape betrayed their bourgeois origins.

Sam was learning wine words. He was seven and he very much enjoyed unnerving adults with his wine-word vocabulary. Hanukkah had just ended and there had been a lot of dinners at Sam's house over the last week, with a lot of wine talk, and Sam had joyfully freaked out a whole table of his relatives by pronouncing after the blessing that the Manischewitz blackberry (the only wine he was allowed to taste) was a "tannacious little cunt of a red, but not without a certain buttery geranium charm." (He finished dinner in his room over that one—but it *was* tannacious. Philistines.)

"You are one of the Chosen?" said a voice up and to the right of Sam. "I destroyed the Canaanites so your people would have a homeland."

He looked up and saw a man with long blond hair wearing a long black duster. A jolt went through Sam like he'd just licked a battery. This was the guy that had scared his friend Josh so badly. He looked around and saw his mom was in the back of the store with Mr. Masterson, the owner.

"Can I get these with this?" asked the man. He had three candy bars in one hand, and a small silver coin about the size of a dime in the other. The coin looked very old.

"That's a foreign coin. I don't think they take it."

The man nodded thoughtfully and looked very sad at the news.

"But Nestlé's Crunch is a fine choice," said Sam, trying to buy time, and keep the guy from going off on him. "A bit naive, but an undergrowth of ambergris and walnut gives it legs."

Sam looked around for his mom again. She was still talking wine with Mr. Masterson, flirting about it—Sam could be cut up in pieces and put away in freezer bags and she wouldn't notice. Maybe he could get the guy to leave.

"Look, they aren't looking. Why don't you just take them?"

"I can't," said the blond man.

"Why not?"

"Because no one has told me to."

Oh no. This guy looked like a grown-up, but actually he had the mind of a dumb little kid inside. Like that guy in *Sling Blade,* or the president.

"Then I'll tell you to, okay?" Sam said. "Go ahead.

Take them. You'd better get going, though. It's going to rain." Sam couldn't remember ever talking to an adult like this before.

The blond man looked at his candy bars, then at Sam. "Thank you. Peace on Earth, goodwill toward men. Merry Christmas."

"I'm Jewish, remember? We don't celebrate Christmas. We celebrate Hanukkah, the miracle of the lights."

"Oh, that wasn't a miracle."

"Sure it was."

"No, I remember. Someone snuck in and put more oil in the lamp. But I will grant a Christmas miracle tomorrow. I must go." With that, the blond man backed away, hugging his candy bars to his chest. "Shalom, child." And in an instant he was just gone.

"Great!" Sam said. "Just great. Throw that in my face!"

Kendra—the Warrior Babe of the Outland, combat mistress of the hot-oil arena, slayer of monsters, menace to mutants, scourge of the sand pirates, sworn protector of the cud-beast herdsmen of Lan, and intramural Blood Champion of the Termite People (mounds seven through twelve inclusive)—enjoyed cheese. So it came to pass, on that twenty-third of December, with her noodles wet and congealing in the colander, that she did raise her well-muscled arm to the sky and call the wrath of all the Furies down upon her higher power, Nigoth the Worm God, for allowing her to leave the mozzarella at the Thrifty-Mart checkout counter. But the gods do not concern themselves in the affairs of lasagna, so the sky did not explode with vengeful fire (or at least not that she could see from the kitchen window) to incinerate the mingy god who would dare desert her in her most dire hour of cheese. What happened was nothing at all.

"Curse be unto you, Nigoth! Would that my blade was not broken, I would track you to the ends of the Outland and sever your thousand and one eyestalks, just to make sure I got your favorite. Then I would feed them raw to the most heinous—"

Then the phone rang.

"Helloo," Molly sang sweetly.

"Molly?" Lena said. "You sound out of breath. Are you okay?"

"Quick, think of something," said the Narrator, *"Don't tell her what you were doing."*

The Narrator had been with Molly almost constantly for the last two days, mostly an irritation, except that he *had* remembered how much oregano and thyme to use in the red sauce. Nevertheless, she knew that he was a sign she needed to get back on her meds ASAP.

"Oh, yeah, I'm fine, Lena. Just buffing the muffin.

You know, gray afternoon, storm coming in, Theo's a mutant—I thought I'd cheer myself up."

There was a long silence on the line, and Molly wondered if she'd sounded convincing.

"Completely convincing," said the Narrator. *"If I wasn't here, I'd swear you were still doing it."*

"You're not here!" Molly said.

"Pardon?" said Lena. "Molly, I can call back if this is a bad time."

"Oh, no, no, no. I'm okay. Just making lasagna."

"I've never heard it called that before."

"For the party."

"Oh, right. How's it going?"

"I forgot the mozzarella. Paid for it, then left it at the checkout stand." She looked at the three cartons of ricotta sitting on the counter, mocking her. Soft cheeses could be so smug.

"I'll go pick it up and bring it over."

"No!" Molly felt a jolt of adrenaline at the thought that she'd have to push through a long girlfriend session with Lena. Things were getting so blurry between Pine Cove and the Outland. "I mean, it's okay. I can do it. I enjoy cheese—shopping for cheese."

Molly heard a sniffle on the other end of the line.

"Mol, I really need to help you with the goddamn lasagna, okay? Really."

"Well, she sounds as nutty as you are," said the Narrator. Molly swatted at the air to shut him up—did a finger-to-lip emphatic rocking shush mime. *"She's a crisis junkie if I ever saw one."*

"I need to talk to someone," Lena said with a sniff. "I broke up with Tucker."

"Oh, I'm so sorry, Lena. Who's Tucker?"

"The pilot I was seeing."

"The guy with the bat? You just met him, didn't you? Take a bath. Eat some ice cream. You've known him two days, right?"

"We shared a lot."

"Cowboy up, Lena. You fucked him and kicked him to the curb. It's not like he stole your design for a cold-fusion reactor. You'll be okay."

"Molly! It's Christmas. You're supposed to be my friend."

Molly nodded at the phone, then realized that Lena couldn't hear her. True, she wasn't being a very good friend. After all, she *was* sworn protector of the cud-beast herdsmen of Lan, as well as a member of the Screen Actors Guild, it was her duty to pretend she cared about her friend's problems.

"Bring the cheese," she said. "We'll be here."

"We?"

"Me. Bring the cheese, Lena."

Theo Crowe showed up at Brine's Bait, Tackle, and Fine Wines just in time to miss everything. Robert Masterson, the owner of Brine's, had called him as soon as he'd seen the mysterious blond man talking to Sam Applebaum, and Theo had rushed right over, only to find that there was nothing to find. The blond guy hadn't hurt or threatened Sam, and the boy seemed fine, except that he kept babbling about changing his religion and becoming a Rastafarian like his cousin Preston who lived on Maui. Theo realized midway through the interview that he was not the guy to enumerate the reasons why one should not spend his life smoking dope and surfing like Sam's cousin Preston because he: (A) had never learned to surf, and (B) didn't have the foggiest idea how Rastafarianism worked, and (C) would eventually have to use the argument: *And look at what a complete loser I am—you don't want that for yourself, do you, Sam?* He left the scene feeling even more useless than he had after the verbal bitch-slapping he'd taken from the pilot at Lena Marquez's house.

When Theo pulled into his driveway at lunchtime, hoping he might be able to patch things up with Molly and get some sympathy and a sandwich, he saw Lena's truck parked in front of the cabin and his heart sank. He debated shuffling over to the commercial pot patch and smoking a sticky bud before going in, but that sounded an awful lot like the behavior of an addict, and he was simply on a little slide from grace, not a blowout. Still, he came through the door humbled, not sure at all how he was going to handle Lena, who might be a murderer, let alone Molly.

"Traitor!" Molly said from over a pan of noodles she was layering into a pan with sauce, meat, and cheese. She had sauce on her hands up to her elbows and looked like she'd been engaged in some very messy surgery. The back door out of the kitchen had slammed shut as he came in.

"Where's Lena?" Theo said.

"She went out the back. Why, are you afraid she'll reveal your secret?"

Theo shrugged and approached his wife, his arms out to the side in a "gimme a break" gesture. Why was it that when she was angry her teeth looked really sharp? He never noticed that any other time. "Mol, I was just doing it so I could get you something for Christmas—I didn't mean to—"

"Oh, I don't care about that—you're investigating Lena. *My friend* Lena. You just went to her house like she's a criminal or something. It's the radiation, isn't it?"

"There's evidence, Molly. And it's not that I got high. I found fruit-bat hairs in Dale's truck and her boyfriend has a fruit bat. And the little Barker kid said—" Theo heard a car start up outside. "I should talk to her."

"Lena wouldn't hurt anyone. She brought me cheese for Christmas, for Christ's sake. She's a pacifist."

"I know that, Molly. I'm not saying that she hurt anyone, but I need to find out—"

"Besides, some fuckers just need killing!"

"Did she tell you—"

"I think it's the pot that makes you reveal your mutant self." She had a lasagna noodle in her hand and was waving it at him. It sort of looked like she was shaking a living creature, but then, he was still a little buzzed.

"Molly, what are you talking about, 'my mutant self'? Are you taking your meds?"

"How dare you accuse me of being crazy. That's worse than if you asked me if it was my time of the month, which it isn't, by the way. But I can't believe that you'd imply that I need to be medicated. You mutant bastard!" She flung the noodle at him and he ducked.

"You *do* need to be medicated, you crazy bitch!" Theo didn't deal well with violence, even in the form of soggy semolina, but after the initial outburst, he immediately lost the will to fight. "I'm sorry, I don't know what I was thinking. Let's just—"

"Fine!" Molly said. She wiped her hands on a dish towel, then tossed it at him. In dodging it, he felt like he was moving in blurred bullet time in the Matrix, but in truth he was just a tall guy who was a little baked and the towel would have missed him anyway. Molly stomped through the little house, into their bedroom, and dropped to the floor on the far side of the bed.

"Molly, you okay?"

She came up holding a package the size of a shoe box wrapped in Christmas paper with a few dust bunnies clinging to it. She held it out to him. "Here. Take it and go. I don't want to see you, traitor. Go."

Theo was stunned. Was she leaving him? Asking him to leave her? How had this gone so wrong so fast?

"I don't want to go. I'm having a really bad day, Molly. I came home hoping to find a little sympathy."

"Yeah? Okay. Here you go. Aw, poor stoned Theo, I'm so sorry that you have to investigate my best friend the day before Christmas Eve when you could be out playing in an illegal pot patch that looks like the jungle plateau of the gibbon people." She held out his present and he took it.

What the hell was she talking about? "So *it is* about the victory garden?"

"Open it," she said.

She didn't say a word more. She put a hand on her hip and fixed him with that "I am so going to kick your ass or fuck your brains out" look that excited and terrified him, as he wasn't always sure which way she would go with it, only that she was going to get satisfaction one way or the other and he was going to be sore the next day because of it. It was a Warrior Babe look, and he realized fully, then, that she was having an episode. She probably really was off her meds. This had to be handled just right.

He backed away a few steps and tore the paper off the package. Inside was a white box with the silver seal of a very exclusive local glassblower, and inside that, wrapped in blue tissue, was the most beautiful bong he'd ever seen. It was like something out of the Art Nouveau era, only fashioned from modern materials, blue-green dichromatic glass with ornate silver branches running through it that gave it the appearance of walking through a forest as he turned it in his hand. The bowl and handle, which fit his hand perfectly, appeared to be cast of solid silver with the same organic tree-branch design seeming to leap right out of the glass. This had to have been made just for him, with his tastes in mind. He felt himself tearing up and blinked back the tears. "It's beautiful."

"Uh-huh," Molly said. "So you can see it's not your garden that bothers me. It's just you."

"Molly, I only want to talk to Lena. Her boyfriend threatened to blackmail me. I was only growing—"

"Take it and go," Molly said.

"Honey, you need to call Dr. Val, maybe see if she'll see you—"

"Get out, goddammit. You don't tell me to see the shrink. Get out!"

It was no use. Not now, anyway. Her voice had hit the Warrior Babe frenzy pitch—he recognized it from the times he'd taken her to the county hospital before they'd become involved as lovers. When she'd just been the town's crazy lady. She'd lose it if he pressed her any more. "Fine. I'll go. But I'll call you, okay?"

She just gave him that look.

"It's Christmas . . ." One last try maybe.

The look.

"Fine. Your present is on the top shelf in the closet. Merry Christmas."

He dug some underwear and socks out of the drawer, grabbed a few shirts out of the closet, and headed out the front door. She slammed it hard enough behind him to break one of the windows. The glass hitting the sidewalk sounded like a summary of his whole life.

Chapter 11

A SLUG TRAIL OF GOOD CHEER

He might have been made of polished mahogany except that when he moved, he moved like liquid. The stage lights reflected green and red off his bald head as he swayed on the stool and teased the strings of a blond Stratocaster with the severed neck of a beer bottle. His name was Catfish Jefferson, and he was seventy, or eighty, or one hundred years old, and not unlike Roberto the fruit bat, he wore sunglasses indoors. Catfish was a bluesman, and on the night before the night before Christmas, he was singing up a forlorn twelve-bar blues fog in the Head of the Slug saloon.

Caught my baby boning Santa,
Underneath the mistletoe (Lawd have mercy).
Caught my baby boning Santa,
Underneath the mistletoe.
Used to be my Christmas angel,
Now she just a Christmas ho.

"I hear dat!" shouted Gabe Fenton. "Sho-nuff, sho-nuff. True dat, my brutha."

Theophilus Crowe looked at his friend, just one in a whole line of awkward, heartbroken men at the bar, rocking almost in rhythm to the beat, and shook his head. "Could you possibly be any whiter?" Theo asked.

"I gots the blues up in me," Gabe said. "She sho-nuff did me wrong."

Gabe had been drinking. Theo, while not quite sober, had not.

(He *had* shared a toothpick-thin spliff of Big Sur polio weed with Catfish Jefferson between sets, the two of them standing in the back parking lot of the Slug, trying to coax fire out of a disposable lighter in a forty-knot wind.)

"Didn't think you muthafuckas had weather here," Catfish croaked, having sucked the joint so far down that the ember looked like the burning eye of a demon staring out of a cave of dark finger and lip. (The calluses on the tips of his fingers were impervious to the heat.)

"El Niño," Theo said, letting loose a blast of smoke.

"Say what?"

"It's a warm ocean current in the Pacific. Comes up the coast every ten years or so. Screws up the fishing, brings torrential rains, storms. They think we might be having an El Niño this year."

"When will they know?" The bluesman had put on his leather fedora and was holding it fast against the wind.

"Usually after everything floods, the wine crop is ruined, and a lot of cliffside houses slide into the ocean."

"And dat because the water too warm?"

"Right."

"No wonder the whole country hate your ass," said Catfish. "Let's go inside fo' my narrow ass gets blowed back to Clarksville."

"It's not that bad," said Theo. "I think it'll blow over."

Winter denial—Theo did it, most Californians did it— they assumed that because the weather was nice most of the time, it would be nice all of the time, and so, in the midst of a rainstorm, you'd find people outdoors without an umbrella, or when nights dipped into the thirties, you'd still see someone dip-pumping his gas in surfer shorts and a tank top. So even as the National Weather

Service was telling the Central Coast to batten down the hatches, as they were about to get the storm of the decade, and even though winds were gusting to fifty knots a full day before the storm made landfall, the people of Pine Cove carried on with their holiday routine like nothing out of the ordinary could happen to them.

Winter denial: therein lay the key to California Schadenfreude—the secret joy that the rest of the country feels at the misfortune of California. The country said: "Look at them, with their fitness and their tans, their beaches and their movie stars, their Silicon Valley and silicone breasts, their orange bridge and their palm trees. God, I hate those smug, sunshiny bastards!" Because if you're up to your navel in a snowdrift in Ohio, nothing warms your heart like the sight of California on fire. If you're shoveling silt out of your basement in the Fargo flood zone, nothing brightens your day like watching a Malibu mansion tumbling down a cliff into the sea. And if a tornado just peppered the land around your Oklahoma town with random trailer trash and redneck nuggets, then you can find a quantum of solace in the fact that the earth actually opened up in the San Fernando Valley and swallowed a whole caravan of commuting SUVs.

Mavis Sand even indulged in a little California Schadenfreude, and she was a Californian born and raised. Secretly, she wished for and enjoyed the forest fires every year. Not so much because she liked watching the state burn down, but because for Mavis's money, there was nothing better than watching a burly man in rubber handling a hefty hose, and during the fires, there were plenty of those on the news.

"Fruitcake?" Mavis said, offering a suspicious slice on a dessert plate to Gabe Fenton, who was drunkenly trying to convince Theo Crowe that he had a genetic predisposition toward the blues, using some impressively large words that no one but he understood, and periodically asking if he could get an "amen" and "five up high," which, as it turned out, he could not.

What he could get was fruitcake.

"Mercy, mercy, my momma done made a fruitcake look just like that," Gabe howled. "Lawd rest her soul."

Gabe reached for the plate, but Theo intercepted it and held it out of the biologist's reach.

"First," Theo said, "your mother was an anthro professor and never baked a thing in her life, and second, she is not dead, and third, you are an atheist."

"Can I get an amen?!" Gabe countered.

Theo raised an eyebrow of accusation toward Mavis.

"I thought we talked about no fruitcake this year."

The prior Christmas, Mavis's fruitcake had put two people into detox. She'd sworn that it would be the last year.

Mavis shrugged. "This cake's nearly a virgin. There's only a quart of rum and barely a handful of Vicodin."

"Let's not," Theo said, handing the plate back.

"Fine," Mavis said. "But get your buddy off his blues jag. He's embarrassing me. And I once blew a burro in a nightclub and wasn't embarrassed, so that's saying something."

"Jeez, Mavis," Theo said, trying to shake the picture from his mind.

"What? I didn't have my glasses on. I thought he was a hirsute insurance salesman with talent."

"I'd better get him home," Theo said, nudging Gabe, who had turned his attention to a young woman on his right who was wearing a low-cut red sweater and had been moving from stool to stool all night long, waiting for someone to talk to her.

"Hi," Gabe said to the woman's cleavage. "I'm not involved in the human experience and I have no re-deeming qualities as a man."

"Me either," said Tucker Case, from the stool on the other side of the red-sweater woman. "Do people keep telling you that you're a psychopath, too? I hate that."

Tucker Case, under several layers of glibness and guile, was actually quite broken up over his breakup with Lena Marquez. It wasn't so much that she had become a part of his life in the two days he had known her, but that she had begun to represent hope. And as the Buddha said: "Hope is merely another face of desire. And desire is a motherfucker." He'd gone out seeking human company to help dilute the disappointment. In another time, he'd have picked up the first woman he encountered, but his man-slut days had left him lonelier than ever, and he would not tread that lubricious path again.

"So," Tuck said to Gabe, "did you just get dumped?"

"She led me on," Gabe said. "She tore my guts out. Evil, thy name is woman!"

"Don't talk to him," Theo said, taking Gabe by the shoulder and unsuccessfully trying to pull him off his bar stool. "This guy's no good."

The young woman sitting between Tuck and Gabe looked from one to the other, then to Theo, then at her breasts, then at the men, as if to say, *Are you guys blind? I've been sitting here all night, with these, and you're going to ignore me.*

Tucker Case *was* ignoring her—well, except for inspecting her sweater cakes as he talked to Gabe and Theo. "Look, Constable, maybe we got off on the wrong foot—"

"Wrong foot?" Theo's voice almost broke. As upset as he appeared, he appeared to be talking to the woman in the red sweater's breasts, rather than to Tucker Case, who was only a foot beyond them. "You threatened me."

"He did?" said Gabe, angling for a better look down

the red sweater. "That's harsh, buddy. Theo just got thrown out of the house."

"Can you believe guys our age can still fall so hard?" Tuck said to Theo, looking up from the cleavage to convey his sincerity. He felt bad about blackmailing Theo, but, much like helping Lena hide the body, sometimes certain unpleasantries needed to be done, and being a pilot and a man of action, he did them.

"What are you talking about?" Theo asked.

"Well, Lena and I have parted ways, Constable. Shortly after you and I spoke this morning."

"Really?" Now Theo looked up from the woolly mounds of intrigue.

"Really," Tuck said. "And I'm sorry things happened the way they did."

"That doesn't really change anything, does it?"

"Would it make a difference if I told you that I absolutely did not harm this alleged Dale Pearson, and neither did Lena?"

"I don't think he was alleged," said Gabe, slurring at the breasts. "I'm pretty sure he was confirmed Dale Pearson."

"Whatever," said Tuck. "Would that change anything? Would you believe that?"

Theo didn't speak right away but appeared to be waiting for an answer from the décolletage oracle. When he looked up at Tuck again he said, "Yeah, I believe you."

Tuck nearly aspirated the ginger ale he was drinking. When he stopped sputtering he said, "Wow, you suck as a lawman, Theo. You can't just believe a strange guy who tells you something in a bar." Tuck wasn't accustomed to being believed by anyone, so to have someone take him at face value . . .

"Hey, hey, hey," said Gabe. "That's uncalled for—"

"Well, fuck you guys!" said the woman in the red sweater. She jumped up from her stool and snatched her keys off the bar. "I am a person, too, you know? And these are not speakerphones," she said, grabbing her breasts underneath and shaking them at the offenders, her keys jingling cheerfully as she did, completely defusing the effect of her anger.

"Oh—my—God," said Gabe.

"You can't just ignore a person like that! Besides, you're all too old and you're losers and I'd rather be alone on Christmas than spend five minutes with any of you horn dogs!" And with that she threw some cash on the bar, turned, and stormed out of the bar.

Because they were men, Theo, Tuck, and Gabe watched her ass as she walked away.

"Too old?" Tuck said. "She was what, twenty-seven, twenty-eight?"

"Yeah," Theo said. "Late twenties, maybe early thirties. I didn't think we were ignoring her."

Mavis Sand took the money off the bar and shook her head. "You were all paying her proper attention. Woman's got some issues when she's jealous of her own parts."

"I was thinking about icebergs," said Gabe. "About how only ten percent of them show above the surface, yet below lies the really dangerous part. Oh, no, I got the blues on me again." His head hit the bar and bounced.

Tuck looked to Theo. "You want some help getting him to the car?"

"He's a very smart guy," said Theo. "He has a couple of Ph.D.s."

"Okay. Do you want some help getting *the doctor* to the car?"

Theo was trying to get a shoulder under Gabe's arm, but given that he was nearly a foot taller than his friend, things weren't working very well.

"Theo," Mavis barked. "Don't be such a friggin' wanker. Let the man help you."

After three unsuccessful attempts at hefting the bag of sand that was Gabe Fenton, Theo nodded to Tuck. They each took an arm and walked/dragged the biologist toward the back door.

"If he hurls I'm aiming him at you," Theo said.

"Lena loved these shoes," said Tuck. "But you do what you feel like you need to."

"I have no sex appeal, a rum-pa-pa-pum," sang Gabe Fenton, in spirit with the season. *"My social skills are nil, a rum-pa-pa-pum."*

"Did that actually rhyme?" asked Tuck.

"He's a bright guy," said Theo.

Mavis creaked ahead of them and held the door. "So, I'll see you pathetic losers at the Lonesome Christmas party, right?"

They stopped, looked at one another, felt camaraderie in their collective loserdom, and reluctantly nodded.

"My lunch is coming up, a rum-pa-pa-pum," sang Gabe.

Meanwhile, the girls were running around the Santa Rosa Chapel, putting up decorations and preparing the table settings for a Lonesome Christmas. Lena Marquez was making her third circumnavigation of the room with a stepladder, some masking tape, and rolls of green and red crepe paper the size of truck tires. (Price Club in San Junipero only sold one size, evidently so you could decorate your entire ocean liner without making two trips.) The act of serial festooning had taken Lena's mind off her troubles, but now the little chapel was starting to resemble nothing more than the nest of a color-blind Ewok. If someone didn't intervene soon the Lonesome Christmas guests would be in danger of being asphyxiated in a festive dungeon of holiday bondage. Fortunately, as Lena was moving the ladder to make her fourth round, Molly Michon snaked a foot inside and pulled the chapel's double doors open; the wind from the growing storm swept in and tore the paper from the walls.

"Well, fuck!" said Lena.

The crepe paper swam in a vortex around the middle of the room, then settled into a great wad under one of the buffet tables Molly had set up to one side.

"I told you a staple gun would work better than masking tape," Molly said. She was holding three stainless-steel pans of lasagna and still managed to get the oak double doors closed against the wind with her feet. She was agile that way.

"This is a historical landmark, Molly. You can't just go shooting staples into the walls."

"Right, like that matters after Armageddon. Take these downstairs to the fridge," Molly said, handing the pans to Lena. "I'll get you the staple gun out of my car."

"What does that mean?" Lena asked. "Do you mean our relationships?"

But Molly had bounded back out through the double doors into the wind. She'd been making more and more cryptic comments like that lately. Like she was talking to someone in the room besides Lena. It was strange. Lena shrugged and headed back to the little room behind the altar and the steps that led downstairs.

Lena didn't like going into the basement of the

chapel. It wasn't really a basement; it was more of a cellar: sandstone walls that smelled of damp earth, a con-
crete floor that had been poured without a vapor barrier
fifty years after the cellar had been dug and so seeped
moisture and formed a fine slime on top in the winter.
Even when the stove was cranked and an electric heater
turned on, it was never warm. Besides, the old, empty
pews stored down there cast shadows that made her feel
as if people were watching her.

"Mmmm, lasagna," said Marty in the Morning, your
drive-time dead guy in the A.M. *"Dudes and dudettes, the
little lady has certainly outdone herself this time. Get a whiff
of that?"*

The graveyard was abuzz with moldy anticipation of
the Lonesome Christmas party.

"It's highly inappropriate, that's what it is," said Esther.
*"I suppose it's better than that horrible Mavis Sand woman
barbecuing again. And how is it that she's still alive, anyway?
She's older than I am."*

"Than dirt, you mean?" said Jimmy Antalvo, whose
faceprint was still embedded in a telephone pole on the
Pacific Coast Highway, where he'd hit it at age nineteen.

"Please, child, if you must be rude, at least be original," said
Malcolm Cowley. *"Don't compound the tedium with cliché."*

*"My wife used to put a layer of hot Italian sausage
between every layer of cheese and noodles,"* said Arthur
Tannbeau. *"Now, that was some good eatin'."*

"Sort of explains the heart attack, too, doesn't it?" said Bess Leander. Being poisoned had left a bitter taste in her mouth that seven years of death could not wash away.

"I thought we agreed not to talk about COD guilt," said Arthur. *"Didn't we agree on that?"* COD was shorthand of the dead for Cause of Death.

"We did agree," said Marty in the Morning.

"I do hope that they sing 'Good King Wenceslas,' " said Esther.

"Shut the fuck up about 'Good King Wenceslas,' would you? No one knows the words to 'Good King Wenceslas,' no one ever has."

"My, my, the new guy is cranky," said Warren Talbot, who had once been a painter of landscapes but after liver failure at seventy was fertilizing one.

"Well, it's gonna be a great party to listen to," said Marty in the Morning. *"Did you hear the constable's wife talking about Armageddon? She's definitely taking a cruise down the Big Nutty."*

"I am not!" shouted Molly, who had come down to the basement to help Lena clear space in the two refrigerators for the salads and desserts that they had yet to unload.

"Who are you talking to?" said Lena, a little frightened at the outburst.

"I think I've made my point," said Marty in the Morning.

Chapter 12

THE STUPIDEST ANGEL'S
CHRISTMAS MIRACLE

Sundown, Christmas Eve. The rain was coming down so hard that there didn't appear to be any space between the drops—just a wall of water, moving almost horizontally on wind that was gusting to seventy miles per hour. In the forest behind the Santa Rosa Chapel, the angel chewed his Snickers and ran a wet hand over the tire tracks at the back of his neck, thinking, *I really should have gotten more specific directions.*

He was tempted to go find the child again and ask him exactly where Santa Claus was buried. He realized now that "somewhere in the woods behind the church" wasn't telling him much. To go back to get directions, however, would dilute somewhat the whole miraculousness of the miracle.

This was Raziel's first Christmas miracle. He'd been passed over for the task for two thousand years, but finally his turn had come up. Well, actually, the Archangel Michael's turn had come up, and Raziel ended up getting the job by losing in a card game. Michael had bet the planet Venus against his assigned task of performing the Christmas miracle this year. Venus! Although he wasn't really sure what he would have done with Venus had he won it, Raziel knew he needed the second planet, if for no other reason than that it was large and shiny.

He didn't like the whole abstract quality of the Christmas miracle mission. "Go to Earth, find a child who has made a Christmas wish that can only be granted by divine intervention, then you will be granted powers to grant that wish." There were three parts. Shouldn't the job be given to three angels? Shouldn't there be a supervisor? Raziel wished he could trade this in for the destruction of a city. That was so simple. You found the city, you killed all the people, you leveled all the buildings, even if you totally screwed it up you could track down the survivors in the hills and kill them with a sword, which, in truth, Raziel kind of enjoyed. Unless, of course, you destroyed the wrong city, and he'd only done that what? Twice? Cities in those days weren't that big, anyway. Enough people to fill a couple of good-size Wal-Marts, tops. *Now there's a mission,* thought the angel: "Raziel! Go forth into the land and lay waste unto two good-size Wal-Marts, slay until blood doth flow from all bargains and all the buildings are but rubble—and pick up a few Snickers bars for yourself."

A tree waving in the wind nearby snapped with the report of a cannon, and the angel came out of his fantasy. He needed to get this miracle done and be gone. Through the rain he could see that people were starting to arrive at the little church, fighting their way through the wind and the rain, the lights in the windows flickering even as the party was starting. There was no going back, the angel thought. He would just have to wing it (which, considering he was an angel, he really should have been better at).

He raised his arms to his sides and his black coat streamed out behind him on the wind, revealing the tips of his wings folded underneath. In his best pronouncement voice, he called out the spell.

"Let he who lies here dead arise!" He sort of did a hand motion to cover pretty much the general area. "Let he who does not live, live again. Arise from your grave this Christmas and live!" Raziel looked at the half-eaten Snickers he was holding and realized that maybe he should be more specific about what was supposed to happen. "Come forth from the grave! Celebrate! Feast!"

Nothing. Nothing whatsoever happened.

There, said the angel to himself. He popped the last of the Snickers bar into his mouth and wiped his hands on his coat. The rain had subsided for a bit and he could see a ways into the woods. Nothing was happening.

"I mean it!" he said in his big scary angel voice.

Not a damn thing. Wet pine needles, some wind, trees whipping back and forth, rain. No miracle.

"Behold!" said the angel. "For I am really not kidding."

A great gust of wind came up at that second and another nearby pine snapped and fell, missing the angel by only a few feet.

"There. It's just going to take a little time."

He walked out of the woods and down Worchester Street into town.

"Wow, I'm famished all of a sudden," said Marty in the Morning, all dead, all the time.

"I know," said Bess Leander, poisoned yet perky. *"I feel really strange. Hungry, and something else. I've never felt this before."*

"*Oh, my dear,*" said Esther, the schoolteacher, "*I can suddenly think of nothing but brains.*"

"*How 'bout you, kid?*" asked Marty in the Morning. "*You thinking about brains?*"

"*Yeah,*" said Jimmy Antalvo. "*I could eat.*"

For Luck, There Is No Chapter 13.

JUST THIS CHRISTMAS PHOTO ALBUM

Sometimes, if you look closely at family snapshots, you can see in the faces of the children, portents of the adults they will become. In the adults, you can sometimes see the face behind the face. Not always, but sometimes . . .

Tucker Case

In this shot we see a well-to-do California family posed in front of their lakeshore estate in Elsinore, California. (It's an eight-by-ten color glossy, embossed with the trademark of a professional photographer's studio.)

They are all tanned and healthy-looking. Tucker Case is perhaps ten years old, dressed in a little sport coat with a yachting ensign on the breast pocket and little tasseled loafers. He is standing in front of his mother, who has the same blond hair and bright blue eyes, the same smile that looks not as if she is presenting her dental work, but as if she is just seconds from bursting out laughing. Three generations of Cases—brothers, sisters, uncles, aunts, and cousins—look perfectly coiffed, pressed, washed, and shined. All are smiling, except for one little girl down front, who has an expression of abject horror on her face.

A closer look reveals the back of her red Christmas dress is tossed up to one side, and snaking in from the side, from under his little blue sport coat, is the hand of young Tuck, who has just stolen an incestuous squeeze of his cousin Janey's eleven-year-old bottom.

What is telling about this picture is not the surreptitious booty grope, but the motive, because here Tucker Case is at an age where he is much more interested in blowing stuff up than he is in sex, yet he is precociously cognizant of just how much his advances will freak his cousin out. This is his raison d'être. It should be noted that Janey Case-Robbins will go on to distinguish herself as a successful litigator and advocate for women's rights, while Tucker Case will go on to be a serially heartbroken horn dog with a fruit bat.

Lena Marquez

The shot is taken in someone's backyard on a sunny day. There are children all around and it's obvious that a big party is going on.

She's six, wearing a fluffy pink dress and patent-leather shoes. She couldn't be any cuter, with her long black hair tied up into ponytails with red ribbons and flying out behind her like silk comet tails as she pursues the piñata. She's blindfolded, and her mouth is wide open, letting forth a burst of that high, little-girl laugh that sounds like joy itself, because she's just made solid contact with the stick and she's sure that she has released candy, and toys, and noisemakers for all the children. What she has, in fact, done, has solidly smacked her uncle Octavio in the *cojones.*

Uncle Octavio is caught in a magic moment of transition, his face changing from joy to surprise to pain, all at once. Lena is still adorable and sweet and unsullied by the disaster she has wrought. *Feliz Navidad!*

Molly Michon

It's Christmas morning, post-present-opening storm. Tissue paper and ribbon are strewn around the floor, and off to one side you can see a coffee table, and on it an ashtray the size of a hubcap overflowing with butts, and an empty bottle of Jim Beam. Front and center is six-year-old Molly Achevski (she would change her last name to Michon at nineteen on the advice of an agent "because it sounds fucking French, people love that"). Molly is wearing a red sequined ballerina outfit, red galoshes that hit her bare legs about midcalf, and a giant, cheeky grin with a hole in the middle where her front teeth used to be. She has one foot propped up on a large Tonka dump truck as if she has just conquered it in a grudge match, and her younger brother Mike, four, is trying to pry the truck out from under her. Tears are streaming down his cheeks. Molly's other brother, Tony, five, is looking up to his sister like she is the princess of all things good. She has already poured him a bowl of Lucky Charms this morning, as she does for both her brothers every morning.

In the background, we see a woman in a bathrobe lying on the couch, one hand hanging to the floor holding a cigarette that has burned itself out hours before. The silvery ash has left a streak on the carpet.

No one has any idea who took this picture.

Dale Pearson

This one was taken only a few years ago, when Dale was still married to Lena. It's the Caribou Lodge Christmas party, and Dale is, once again, dressed as Santa, sitting on a makeshift throne. He is surrounded by drunken revelers, all laughing, all holding the various joke gifts that Dale has passed out to them earlier that night. Dale is brandishing his own present, a fourteen-inch-long rubber penis, as big around as a soup can. He's waving it at Lena with a leer, and she, dressed in a black cocktail dress and a single string of pearls, looks quite horrified at what he's saying, which is: "We'll put this rascal to good use later tonight, huh, baby?"

The irony of it is that later that night, he will don one of his vintage German SS uniforms—everything but the jodhpurs, anyway—and what he asks Lena to do with his new present is exactly what she told him he could do with it at the party. She will never know if it was she who gave him the idea, but it will be a milestone in her move toward divorce proceedings.

Theophilus Crowe

At thirteen, Theo Crowe is already six feet four inches tall, and weighs a little over a hundred pounds. It is a classic scene of the three kings following the star. The seventh-grade music class is performing *Amahl and the Night Visitors.* Originally cast as one of the three kings, Theo is now dressed as a camel. His ears are the only parts of his body that are in proportion, and he looks very much like a camel fashioned out of wire by Salvador

Dalí. His chance to play Balthazar, the Ethiopian king, was lost when he announced that the Magi had arrived bearing gold, *Frankenstein,* and myrrh. Later, he, the two other camels, and a sheep will be suspended for smoking the myrrh. (They would have never been caught had the sheep not suggested that they play a quick game of "Kill the Man with the Baby Jesus" out behind the theater. Evidently the myrrh was "prime smokage.")

Gabe Fenton

This one was taken just last year, at the lighthouse where Gabe has his cabin. You can see the lighthouse in the background, and windblown whitecaps out to sea. You can tell it's a windy day because the Santa hat that Gabe is wearing is streaming out to the side, and he's holding the reindeer antlers on Skinner's head. Crouched next to them, in a thousand-dollar St. John knit, red and cut in the style of a Napoleonic soldier, with brass buttons and gold braid on the shoulders, is Dr. Valerie Riordan. Her auburn hair is styled to curl behind her ears and accentuate her diamond hoop earrings. She's done up in Headline News Prompter Puppet makeup, as if her face has been completely sanded off, and then painted back on by a crack team of special-effects people—brighter, better, faster than a real human face. She's trying, really trying, to smile for the camera. She is holding her hair in one hand, and appears to be petting Skinner, but is, upon closer examination, holding him at bay. A racing stripe across the knee of her nylons betrays an earlier attempt by Skinner to share a holiday leg hump with the Food Guy's female.

Gabe is scruffy in khakis and hiking boots. There's a fine coating of sand on his pants and boots from where he was sitting astride elephant seals that morning, gluing satellite-tracking devices on their backs. He has a great, hopeful smile, and not a clue that anything might be wrong with this picture.

Roberto T. Fruit Bat

This picture was taken on the island of Guam, Roberto's birthplace. There are palm trees in the foreground. You can tell he's just a young fellow, because he has not yet acquired a pair of Ray·Bans, nor a master to bring him mangoes on demand. He's curled up in a Christmas wreath made from palm fronds and decorated with little papayas and red palm nuts. He is licking papaya pulp from his little doggy face. The children who found him in the wreath that Christmas morning are posed on either side of the door where the wreath hangs. They are both girls, and have the long curly brown hair of their Chamorro mother, the green eyes of their Irish-Catholic father, who is an American airman. Father is taking the picture. The girls are in bright, floral mission dresses with puffy sleeves.

Later, after church, they will try to coax Roberto into a box so they can later cook him and serve him with saimen noodles. Although he escapes, the incident traumatizes the young bat and he does not speak for years.

Chapter 14

THE CAMARADERIE OF
THE LONESOME CHRISTMAS

Theo wore his cop shirt to the Lonesome Christmas party. Not because he didn't have anything else to wear, because there were still two clean flannels and a Phish sweatshirt in the Volvo that he'd snagged from the cabin, but because with the storm pounding the stuffing out of Pine Cove, he felt as if he should be doing cop stuff. His cop shirt had epaulets on the shoulders (that are used for, uh, holding your paulets—no—for keeping your hat under—for your parrot to stand on—no) that looked cool and military, plus it had a little slot in the pocket where he could pin his badge and another one where he could stick a pen, which could be really handy in a storm in case you wanted to take notes or some-thing, like: 7 *P.M., Still Really Fucking Windy.*

"Wow, it's really fucking windy," Theo said. It was 7 P.M.

Theo stood in the corner of the main room of the Santa Rosa Chapel next to Gabe Fenton, who was wearing one of his science shirts: a khaki canvas utility shirt with many pockets, slots, buttons, pouches, epaulets, zippers, Velcro loops, snaps, and vents, so you could hopelessly lose everything you owned in it and essen-tially sand your nipples off while patting the pockets and saying, "I know I had it here somewhere."

"Yep," Gabe said. "It was gusting to a hundred and twenty when I left the lighthouse."

"You're kidding! A hundred and twenty miles per hour? We're all going to die," Theo said, feeling sud-denly better.

"Kilometers per hour," Gabe said. "Stand in front of me. She's looking." He snagged Theo by the epaulet (aha!) and pulled him around to block the view from the other side of the room. Across the open hardwood floor, Valerie Riordan, in charcoal Armani over red Ferra-gamos, was sipping a cranberry and soda from a plastic cup.

"Why's she here?" Gabe whispered. "Didn't she get a better offer from some country club or some business guy or something?" Gabe said the word *business* like it was a putrid taste that he needed to spit out before it sickened him, which was exactly how he meant it. Although Gabe did not live in an ivory tower, he did live next to one, and it gave him a skewed perspective on commerce.

"Your eye is twitching really badly, Gabe. Are you okay?"

"I think it's conditioning from the electrodes. She looks so great, don't you think?"

Theo looked over at Gabe's ex-girlfriend, considered the heels, the stockings, the makeup, the hair, the lines of her suit, her nose, her hips, and felt like he was looking at a sports car that he could not afford, would not know how to drive, and he could only envision himself entangled in the wreckage of, wrapped around a telephone pole.

"Her lipstick matches her shoes," Theo said, by way of not really answering his friend. That sort of thing didn't happen in Pine Cove. Well, Molly did have some black lipstick that matched a pair of black boots she had, which she wore with nothing else, but he really didn't want to think about that. In fact, this moment would only have any meaning at all when he shared it with Molly, which he realized he wasn't going to be doing, which made him jealous of Gabe's twitch for a second.

The double doors to the chapel opened, and wind whipped through the room, rattling the few strands of crepe paper that still clung to the wall to this point and knocking a couple of ornaments off the giant Christmas tree. Tucker Case came in, his bomber jacket dripping, a little furry face sticking out through the V in the zipper in the front.

"No dogs," said Mavis Sand, who was fighting to get the doors shut. "We've just let kids come the last couple of years, and I'm not happy about it."

Tuck grabbed the other door and pulled it shut, then reached over Mavis and caught the door she was battling. "He's not a dog."

Mavis turned around and looked right into the face of Roberto, who made a little barking sound. "That's a dog. Not much of a goddamn dog, I'll give you that, but a dog. And he's wearing sunglasses."

"So?"

"It's dark, moron. Get rid of the dog."

"He's not a dog," Tuck said, and to illustrate his point, he unzipped his jacket, took Roberto by the feet, and flung him at the ceiling. The bat yelped, opened his leathery wings, and flew to the top of the Christmas tree, where he caught the star, swung halfway around, and settled, upside down, hanging there above the room, looking, despite his cheery nature and hot pink sunglasses, a little creepy.

Everyone in the place, thirty or so people, stopped whatever they were doing and looked. Lena Marquez, who had been cutting lasagna into squares over at the buffet table, looked up, made brief eye contact with Tuck, then looked away. Except for the boom box playing reggae Christmas carols and the wind and rain thrashing outside, there was not a sound.

"What?" Tuck said to everyone and no one in particular. "You people act like you've never seen a bat before."

"Looked like a dog," Mavis said from behind him.

"You don't have a no-bat policy, then?" Tuck said, not turning around.

"Don't think so. You got a great ass, flyboy, you know that?"

"Yeah, it's a curse," Tuck said. He eyed the ceiling for any mistletoe he might get trapped under, spotted Theo and Gabe, then made a beeline for the corner where they were hiding.

"Oh my God," said Tuck as he was approaching. "Did you guys see Lena? She's so hot. Don't you think she's hot? I miss her."

"Oh God, not you, too," Theo said.

"That Santa hat, it does something to me."

"That a *Pteropus tokudae*?" asked Gabe, peeking out quickly from behind Theo and nodding toward the Christmas tree with the bat.

"No, that's Roberto. Why are you hiding behind the constable?"

"My ex is here."

Tuck looked over. "The redhead in the suit?"

Gabe nodded.

Tuck looked at him, back at Val Riordan, who was now chatting with Lena Marquez, then again at Gabe. "Whoa, you were really crawling out of your gene pool, huh? Let me shake your hand." He reached around Theo, offering his hand to the biologist.

"We don't like you, you know?" Theo said.

"Really?" Tuck took his hand back. He looked around Theo at Gabe. "Really?"

"You're okay," said Gabe. "He's just cranky."

"I am not cranky," Theo said, but, in fact, he was a little cranky. A little sad. A little stoned. A little out of sorts that this storm hadn't just blown over like he'd hoped, and a little excited that it might actually turn into a disaster. Secretly, Theophilus Crowe loved a disaster.

"Understandable," Tuck said, squeezing Theo's shoulder. "Your wife was a biscuit."

"Is a biscuit," corrected Theo, but then, "Hey!"

"No, it's okay," Tuck said. "You were a lucky man."

Gabe Fenton reached up and squeezed Theo's other shoulder. "It's true," Gabe said. "When Molly isn't completely off her rocker, she *is* a biscuit. Actually, even when she is—"

"Would you guys quit calling my wife a biscuit! I don't even know what that means."

"Something we say in the islands," Tuck said. "What I'm saying is, you've got nothing to be ashamed of. You guys had a good run. You can't expect her to lose her sense of judgment forever. You know, Theo, every now and then Eraserhead will hook up with Tinker Bell, or Sling Blade Carl will marry Lara Croft—that sort of thing gives us hope—but you can't count on it. You can't bet that way. Why, guys like us would always be alone if some women didn't have a deep-seated streak of self-destruction, isn't that right, Professor?"

"Truth," said Gabe. He made a sort of swear-on-the-Bible gesture. Theo glared at him.

"Eventually a woman will wise up," Tuck continued.

"She's just gone off her meds."

"Whatever," Tuck said. "I'm just saying that it's Christmas and you should be grateful that you were ever able to fool someone into loving you in the first place."

"I'm calling her," Theo said. He pulled his cell phone from the pocket of his cop shirt and keyed the button for his home number.

"Is Val wearing the pearl earrings?" Gabe asked. "I bought her those."

"Diamonds studs," said Tuck, checking over his shoulder.

"Dammit."

"Look at Lena in that Santa hat. That woman has a talent with tinsel, if you know what I mean?"

"No idea," said Gabe.

"Me either. It just sounded kinky," said Tuck.

Theo snapped the cell phone shut. "I hate both you guys."

"Do not," said Tuck.

"No service?" asked Gabe.

"I'm going to see if the police radio in my car is working."

Rain was pooling in the graveyard behind the chapel as the dead pulled one another from the muck.

"This looked easier in the movies," said Jimmy Antalvo, who was waist-deep in a puddle and being pulled out by Marty in the Morning and the new guy in the red suit. Jimmy's words were a little slurred and slurpy, between the mud and a facial structure that was mostly mortician's wax and wire. "I thought I'd never get out of that coffin."

"Kid, you're better off than a couple we've pulled out," said Marty in the Morning. He nodded to a very feeble and mostly decomposed pile of animated meat that had at one time been an electrician. The mushy thing made a moaning sound.

"Who's that?" asked Jimmy. The torrential rain had washed the mud out of his eyes.

"That's Alvin," said Marty. "All we can understand from him."

"I used to talk to him all the time," said Jimmy.

"It's different now," said the guy in the red suit. "Now you're really talking, not just thinking it. His talking equipment is past warranty."

Marty, who had been portly in life but had slimmed down significantly since his death, bent down and got a good grip on Jimmy's arm, bending the elbow around his own, then made a great straining lift to pull the kid out. There was a loud pop and Marty went over backward into the mud. Jimmy Antalvo was waving around an empty leather jacket sleeve and yelling, "My arm! My arm!"

"Jeez, they should have sewn that on better," said Marty, holding the arm in the air, even as the hand appeared to be doing a very jerky version of a parade wave.

"This whole undead rigmarole is disgusting," said Esther, the schoolteacher, who was standing to the side with a few others who had already been dug up. Water was pouring off the shreds of her best church dress, which had been reduced by time to calico tatters. "I'll not have anything to do with it."

"So you're not hungry?" said the new guy, muddy rainwater streaming out of his Santa beard. He'd been the first one out, since he hadn't had to escape a coffin.

"Fine, once we get the kid out we'll just push you back down your hole."

"I'm not saying that," said Esther. "I would enjoy a snack. Something light. Mavis Sand, maybe. That woman can't have enough brains to spread on a cracker."

"Then shut up and help us get everyone out."

Nearby, Malcolm Cowley was staring disapprovingly at one of the less articulate members of the undead who had been pulled from his grave and was showing lots of bare bone between the meat. The dead book dealer was wringing out his tweed jacket and shaking his head at every comment. "Suddenly we are all gluttons, are we? Well, I have always enjoyed Danish Modern furniture for its functional yet elegant design, so once we have consumed the brains of these revelers, I feel compelled to seek out one of these furniture boutiques I have heard so much about from newlyweds in the chapel. First we feast, then IKEA."

"IKEA," chanted the dead. "First we feast, then IKEA. First we feast, then IKEA."

"Can I eat the constable's wife's brain?" asked Arthur Tannbeau. "She sounds like she'll be spicy—"

"Get everyone out of the ground, then we eat," said the new guy, who was used to telling people what to do.

"Who died and made you boss?" asked Bess Leander.

"All of you," answered Dale Pearson.

"The man has a point," said Marty in the Morning.

"I think while you boys finish up here, I'll have a stroll around the parking lot. Oh my, I don't seem to be walking very well," said Esther, dragging one foot behind her and plowing a furrow in the mud as she moved. "But IKEA does sound like a delightful after-supper adventure."

No one knows why, but second only to eating the brains of the living, the dead love affordable prefab furniture.

Across the parking lot, Theophilus Crowe was busy having the water in his ears replaced with dog spit.

"Get down, Skinner." Theo pushed the big dog away and keyed the mike on the police radio. He had been adjusting the squelch and the gain, and getting little more than distant disembodied voices, just a word here or there in the static. The rain on the car was so loud that Theo put his head down by the dash to better hear the little speaker, and Skinner, of course, took this as an invitation to lick more rain out of Theo's ears.

"Ack! Skinner." Theo grabbed the dog muzzle and steered it between the seats. It wasn't the dampness, or even the dog breath, which was considerable, it was the noise. It was just too loud. Theo dug into the console between the seats and found half a Slim Jim in a folded-over wrapper. Skinner inhaled the tiny meat stick and

198   CHRISTOPHER MOORE

savored the greasy goodness by smacking his chops right next to Theo's ear.

Theo snapped the radio off. One of the problems with living in Pine Cove, with the ubiquitous Monterey pines, was that after a few years the Christmas trees stopped looking like Christmas trees and started looking like giant upturned dust mops, a great sail of needles and cones at the top of a long, slender trunk and a pancake root system—a tree especially adapted to fall over in high wind. So when El Niño cruised up the coast and storms like this came in, first cell and cable TV repeater stations lost power, soon the town lost its main power, and finally, phone lines would go down, effectively cutting all communications. Theo had seen it before, and he didn't like what it portended. Cypress Street would be underwater before dawn and people would be kayaking through the real-estate offices and art galleries by noon.

Something hit the car. Theo turned on the headlights, but the rain was coming down so hard and the windows were so fogged with dog breath that he could see nothing. He assumed it was a small tree branch. Skinner barked, deafeningly loud in the enclosed space.

He could go patrolling downtown, but with Mavis having closed the Slug for Christmas Eve, he couldn't imagine why anyone would be down there. Go home? Check on Molly? Actually, she was better equipped with her little four-wheel-drive Honda to drive in this mess, and she was smart enough to stay home in the first place. He was trying not to take it personally that she hadn't come to the party. Trying not to take to heart the pilot's words about not being worthy of a woman like her.

He looked down, and there, cradled in bubble wrap in the console, was the art-glass bong. Theo picked it up, looked it over, then pulled a film can of sticky green buds from his cop-shirt pocket and began loading the pipe.

Theo was briefly blinded by the spark of the disposable lighter, at the same time as something scraped against the car. Skinner jumped over into the front seat and barked at the window, his hefty tail beating against Theo's face.

"Down, boy. Down," Theo said, but the big dog was now digging at the vinyl panel on the door. Knowing that it meant that he'd have to deal with a lot of wet dog later, but feeling that he really needed to get a buzz on in peace, Theo reached over and threw open the passenger door. Skinner bounded out the door. The wind slammed it behind him.

There was a commotion outside, but Theo could see nothing, and he figured that Skinner was just frisking in the mud. The constable lit the bong and lost himself in the scuba bubbles of sweet comforting smoke.

Outside the car, not ten feet away, Skinner was gleefully tearing the head off an undead schoolteacher. Her arms and legs were flailing and her mouth was moving, but the retriever had already bitten through the better part of her decayed throat and was shaking her head back and forth in his jaws. A skilled lip-reader would have been able to tell you that Esther was saying: "I was only going to eat a little of his brain. This is entirely un-called for, young man."

I am so going to get bad-dogged for this, Skinner thought.

Theo stepped out of the car into an ankle-deep puddle. Despite the cold, the wind, the rain, and the mud that had squished over the edge of his hiking boots, Theo sighed, for he was sorely, wistfully stoned, and slipping into that comfortable place where everything, including the rain, was his fault and he'd just have to live with it. Not a maudlin self-pity that might have come from Irish whiskey, nor an angry tequila blame, nor a jittery speed paranoia, just a little melancholy self-loathing and the realization of what a total loser he was.

"Skinner. Get over here. Come on, boy, back in the car."

Theo could barely see Skinner, but the big dog was on his back rolling in something that looked like a pile of wet, muddy laundry—sort of snaking back and forth with his mouth open and his pink tongue whipping around in ecstatic dogasm.

Probably a dead raccoon, Theo thought, trying to blink some rain out of his eyes. *I've never been that happy. I will never be that happy.*

He left the dog to his joy and slogged back into the Lonesome Christmas. He thought he felt a hand across his neck as he wrestled his way through the double doors, then a loud moan when the doors slammed shut, but it was probably just the wind. It didn't feel like the wind. Had to be the wind.

Chapter 15

A MOMENTARY FLASH OF MOLLY

"By the purple horn of Nigoth, I command thee to boil!" screeched the Warrior Babe. What good was a higher power, after all, if he wouldn't help you cook your ramen noodles? Molly stood over the stove, naked, except for a wide sash from which was slung the scabbard for her broadsword at the center of her back, giving the impression that she had won honors in the Miss Nude Random Violence Pageant. Her skin was slick with sweat, not because she'd been working out, but because she'd chopped up the coffee table with her broken broadsword and burned it, along with two chairs from the dining-room set, in the fireplace. The cabin was sweltering. The power hadn't gone out yet, but it would soon, and the Warrior Babe of the Outland dropped into survival mode a little sooner than most people. It was in her job description.

"It's Christmas Eve," said the Narrator. *"Shouldn't we eat something more festive? Eggnog? How about sugar cookies in the shape of Nigoth? Do you have purple sprinkles?"*

"You'll get nothing and like it! You are but a soulless ghost that vexes me and stirs in my mind like spiders. When my check arrives on the fifth, you shall be banished to the abyss forever."

"I'm just saying, hacking up the coffee table? Screaming at the soup? I think you could channel your energies in a more positive way. Something in the holiday spirit."

In a momentary flash of Molly, the Warrior Babe realized that there was a line she could cross, when the Narrator actually became the voice of reason, as opposed to a niggling voice trying to get her to act out. She turned the burner down to medium and went to the bedroom.

She pulled a stool over to the closet and climbed up on it so she could reach to the back shelf. The problem with marrying a guy who was six foot six, is you often find yourself scaling the counters to get to stuff that he placed there for convenience. That, and you needed a riding steam iron in order to press one of his shirts. Not that she did that very often, but if you try to get a crease straight in a forty-inch sleeve once, you're as likely as not to give up ironing altogether. She was nuts already, she didn't need help from trying to perform frustrating tasks.

After feeling around on the top shelf, brushing over the spare holster for Theo's Glock, her hand closed on a velvet-wrapped bundle. She climbed down from the stool and took the long bundle to the couch, where she sat down and slowly unwrapped it.

The scabbard was made of wood. Somehow it had been laminated with layers of black silk, so that it appeared to drink the light out of the room. The handle was wrapped in black silk cord and there was a cast bronze hand guard with a filigreed dragon design. The ivory head of a dragon protruded from the pommel. When she pulled the sword from the scabbard, her breath caught in her throat. She knew immediately that it was real, it was ancient, and it had to have been exorbitantly expensive. It was the finest blade she had ever seen in person, and a *tashi,* not a *katana.* Theo knew she would want the longer, heavier sword for working out, that she would spend hours training with this valuable antique, not lock it in a glass case to be looked at.

Tears welled up in her eyes and the blade turned to a silver blur in her vision. He had risked his freedom and his pride to buy her this, to acknowledge that part of her that everyone else seemed to want to get rid of.

"Your soup is boiling over," said the Narrator, *"you sentimental sissy-girl."*

And it was. She could hear the hiss of the water hitting the hot burner. Molly leaped to her feet and looked around for a place to set the sword. The coffee table had long since gone to ash in the fireplace. She looked to the bookshelf under the front window, and in that second there was a deafening snap as the trunk of a big pine gave way outside, followed by lighter crackles and snaps as it took out branches and smaller trees on the way to the ground. Sparks lit up the night outside, and the lights went out as the entire cabin shook with the impact of the tree hitting in the front yard. Molly could see the downed power lines out by the road arcing orange and blue through the night. Silhouetted in the window was a tall dark figure, standing there, just looking at her.

Although a lot of single people attended, the Lonesome Christmas party was never supposed to have been a pickup scene, an extension of the holiday musical chairs that went on at the Head of the Slug. People did occasionally meet there, become lovers, mates, but that wasn't the purpose. Originally it was just a get-together for people who had no family or friends in the area with whom to spend Christmas, and who didn't want to spend it alone, or in an alcohol-induced coma, or both. Over the years it had become somewhat more—an anticipated event that people actually chose to attend instead of more traditional gatherings with friends and family.

"I can't imagine a more heinous horror show than spending the holidays with my family," said Tucker Case as Theo rejoined the group. "How about you, Theo?"

There was another guy standing with Tuck and Gabe, a balding blond guy who looked like an athlete gone to fat, wearing a red Star Fleet Command shirt and dress slacks. Theo recognized him as Joshua Barker's stepfather/mom's boyfriend/whatever, Brian Henderson.

"Brian," Theo said, remembering the guy's name at the last second and offering his hand. "How are you? Are Emily and Josh here?"

"Uh, yeah, but not with me," Brian said. "We sort of had a falling-out."

Tucker Case stepped in. "He told the kid that there was no Santa Claus and that Christmas was just a brilliant scheme cooked up by retailers to sell more stuff. What else was it? Oh yeah, that Saint Nicholas was originally famous because he brought back to life some children who'd been dismembered and stuffed into a pickle jar. The kid's mom threw him out."

"Oh, sorry," Theo said.

Brian nodded. "We hadn't been getting along that well."

"He sort of fits right in with us," Gabe said. "Check out the cool shirt."

Brian shrugged, a little embarrassed. "It's red. I thought it would be Christmasy. Now I feel—"

"Ha," Gabe interrupted. "Don't worry about it. The guys in the red shirts never make it to the second commercial break." He punched Brian gently in the arm in a gesture of nerd solidarity.

"Well, I'm going to run out to the car and grab another shirt," said Brian. "I feel silly. I have all my clothes in the Jetta. Everything I own, really."

As Brian walked toward the door, Theo suddenly remembered. "Oh, Gabe, I forgot. Skinner got out of the car. He's rolling in something foul out there in the mud. Maybe you should go with Brian and see if you can get him back in the car."

"He's a water dog. He'll be fine. He can stay out until the party is over. Maybe he'll jump up on Val with muddy paws. Oh, I hope, I hope, I hope."

"Wow, that's kinda bitter," Tuck said.

"That's because I'm a bitter little man," Gabe said. "In my spare time, I mean. Not all the time. My work keeps me pretty busy."

Brian had skulked away in his *Star Trek* shirt. As he

opened one side of the double doors, the wind caught the door and whipped it back against the outside church wall with a gunshot report. Everyone turned to watch the big man shrug sheepishly, and Skinner, muddy and wet to the core, came trotting in, carrying something in his jaws.

"Wow, he's really tracking in a mess," Tuck said. "I never realized the perks of having a flying mammal as a pet before."

"What's that he's carrying in his mouth?" asked Theo.

"Probably a pinecone," Gabe said without looking. Then he looked. "Or not."

There was a scream, a long protracted one, that started with Valerie Riordan and sort of passed through all the women near the buffet. Skinner had presented his prize to Val, dropped it on her foot, in fact, thinking that because she was standing near food, and she was still the Food Guy's female (for who could think of food without thinking of the Food Guy?), she would, therefore, appreciate it, and perhaps reward him. She didn't.

"Grab him!" Gabe yelled to Val, who looked up at him with the most articulate glare he had ever seen. Perhaps it was the weight of her M.D. that gave it eloquence, but without a word, it said: *You have got to be out of your fucking mind.*

"Or not," Gabe said.

Theo crossed the room and made a grab for Skinner's collar, but at the last second the Lab grabbed the arm, threw a head fake, then ducked out of Theo's reach. The three men started to give chase, and Skinner frisked back and forth across the pine floor, his head high and proud as a Lippizaner stallion, pausing occasionally to shake a spray of mud onto the horrified onlookers.

"Tell me it's not moving," shouted Tuck, trying to cut Skinner off at the buffet table. "That hand is not moving."

"Just the kinetic energy of the dog moving through the arm," said Gabe, having gone into a sort of wrestling stance. He was used to catching animals in the wild and knew that you had to be nimble and keep your center of gravity low and use a lot of profanity. "Goddammit, Skinner, come here. Bad dog, bad dog!"

Well, there it was. Tragedy. A thousand trips to the vet, a grass-eating nausea, a flea you will never, ever reach. *Bad dog.* For the love of Dog! He was a bad dog. Skinner dropped his prize and assumed the tail-tucked posture of absolute humility, shame, remorse, and overt sadness. He whimpered and ventured a look at the Food Guy, a sideways glance, pained but ready, should another BD come his way. But the Food Guy wasn't even looking at him. No one was even looking at him. Everything was fine. He was good. Were those sausages he smelled over by that table? Sausages are good.

"That thing is moving," Tuck said.

"No, it's not. Oh, yes it is," said Gabe.

There was another series of screams, this time a couple of man-screams among the women and children. The hand was trying to crawl away, dragging the arm along behind it.

"How fresh does that have to be to do that?" Tuck asked.

"That's not fresh," said Joshua Barker, one of the few kids in the room.

"Hi, Josh," said Theo Crowe. "I didn't see you come in."

"You were out in your car hitting a bong when we got here," Josh said cheerfully. "Merry Christmas, Constable Crowe."

"'Kay," Theo said. Thinking fast, or what seemed like it was fast, Theo took off his Gore-Tex cop coat and threw it over the twitching arm. "Folks, it's okay. I have a little confession to make. I should have told you all before, but I couldn't believe my own observations. It's time I was honest with you all." Theo had gotten very good at telling embarrassing things about himself at Narcotics Anonymous meetings, and confession seemed to be coming even easier since he was a little baked. "A few days ago I ran into a man, or what I thought was a man, but was actually some kind of indestructible cybernetic robot. I hit him doing about fifty in my Volvo, and he didn't even seem to notice."

"The Terminator?" asked Mavis Sand. "I'd fuck him."

"Don't ask me how he got here, or what he really is. I think we've all learned over the years that the sooner we accept the simple explanation for the unexplained, the better chance we have of surviving a crisis. Anyway, I think that this arm may be part of that machine."

"Bullshit!" came a shout from outside the front doors.

Just then the doors flew open, the wind whipped into the room carrying with it a horrid stench. Standing there, framed in the cathedral doorway, stood Santa Claus, holding Brian Henderson in his red *Star Trek* shirt, by the throat. A group of dark figures were moving behind them, moaning something about IKEA, as Santa pressed a .38 snub-nose revolver to Brian's temple and pulled the trigger. Blood splattered across the front wall and Santa threw the body back to Marty in the Morning, who began to suck the brains out of dead Brian's exit wound.

"Merry Christmas, you doomed sons a' bitches!" said Santa.

Chapter 16

SO . . .

So that sucked.

Chapter 17

HE KNOWS IF YOU'VE BEEN
BAD OR GOOD . . .

While she was horrified by what was going on in the doorway of the chapel, with the gunfire and brain-sucking and the threats, Lena Marquez couldn't help but think: *Oh, this is so awkward—both my exes are here.* Dale was standing there in a Santa suit, mud and gore dripping onto the floor while he roared with anger, and Tucker Case had immediately headed to the back of the room and dived under one of the folding buffet tables.

There was screaming and a lot of running, but mostly people stood there, paralyzed by the shock. And Tucker Case, of course, was acting the consummate coward. She was so ashamed.

"You, bitch!" dead Dale Pearson shouted, pointing at

her with the snub-nose .38. "You're lunch!" He started across the open pine floor.

"Look out, Lena," came a shout from behind her. She turned just in time to sidestep as the buffet table behind her rose, spilling chafing dishes full of lasagna onto the floor. The alcohol burners beneath the pans spilled blue flame across the tabletops and onto the floor as Tucker Case stood up with the table in front of him and let out a war cry.

Theo Crowe saw what was happening and pulled an armload of people aside as Tuck barreled through the room, the tabletop in front of him, toward the throng of undead. Dale Pearson fired at the tabletop as it approached, getting off three shots before Tuck impacted with him.

"Crowe, get the door, get the door," Tuck shouted, driving Dale and his undead followers back out into the rain. The blue alcohol flame climbed up Dale's white beard, as well as spilling down Tuck's legs as he pushed out into the darkness. Theo loped across the room and reached outside to catch the edge of the door. A one-armed corpse in a leather jacket ducked around the edge of Tuck's buffet-table barrier and grabbed at Theo, who put a foot on the corpse's chest and drove him back down the steps. Theo pulled the door shut, then reached around and grabbed the other one. He hesitated.

"Close the damned door!" Tuck screamed, his legs pumping, losing momentum against the undead as he reached the bottom of the steps. Theo could see decayed hands clawing at Tuck over the edge of the table; a man whose lower jaw flapped on a slip of skin was screeching at the pilot and trying to drive his upper teeth into Tuck's hand.

The last thing Theo saw as he pulled the door shut was Tucker Case's legs burning blue and steaming in the rain.

"Bring one of those tables over here," Theo shouted. "Brace this door. Jam the table under the handles."

There was a second of peace, just the sound of the wind and rain and Emily Barker, who had just seen her ex-boyfriend shot and brain-sucked, sobbing.

"What was that?" shouted Ignacio Nuñez, a rotund Hispanic who owned the village nursery. "What in the hell was that?"

Lena Marquez had instinctively gone to Emily Barker, and knelt with her arm around the bereft woman. She looked to Theo. "Tucker is out there. He's out there."

Theo Crowe realized that everyone was looking at him. He was having trouble catching his breath and he could feel his pulse pounding in his ears. He really wanted to look to someone else for the answers, but as he scanned the room—some forty terrified faces—he saw all the responsibility reflected back to him.

"Oh fuck," he said, his hand falling to his hip where his holster was usually clipped.

"It's on the table at my house," Gabe Fenton said. Gabe was holding the buffet table that was braced sideways under the double latches of the church doors.

"Pull the table," Theo said, thinking, *I don't even like the guy.* He helped Gabe pull the table aside and crouched in a sprinter's stance, ready to go, as Gabe manned the latches.

"Close it behind me. When you hear me scream, 'Let me in,' well—"

Just then there was a crash behind them and something came flying through one of the high, stained-glass windows—throwing glass out into the middle of the room. Tucker Case, wet, charred, and covered with blood, pushed himself up from the floor where he had landed and said, "I don't know who parked under that window, but you'd better move your car, because if those things climb on it, they'll be coming through that window behind me."

Theo looked at the line of stained-glass windows running down the sides of the chapel, eight on each side, each about eight feet off the ground and about two feet across. When the chapel had been built, stained glass was at a premium and the community poor, thus the small, high windows, which were going to be an asset in defending this place. There was only one large window in the whole building—behind where the altar used to stand, but where now stood Molly's thirty-foot Christmas tree—a six-by-ten-foot large cathedral-shaped stained-glass depiction of Saint Rose, patron saint of interior decorators, presenting a throw pillow to the Blessed Virgin.

"Nacho," Theo barked to Ignacio Nuñez, "see if you can find something in the basement to board up that window."

As if on cue, two muddy, decaying faces appeared at the opening through which Tuck had just dived, moaning and trying to get purchase on the windowsill with their skeletal hands to climb in.

"Shoot them!" Tuck screamed from the floor. "Shoot those fucking things, Theo!"

Theo shrugged, shook his head. No gun.

Something flashed by Theo and he spun to see Gabe Fenton running hell-bent-for-leather at the window, holding before him a long stainless-steel pan full of lasagna, evidently intent upon diving through the window in a pastafarian act of self-sacrifice. Theo caught the biologist by the collar, stopping him like a running dog at the end of his leash. His arms and legs flew out before him and he managed to hang on to the pan, but nearly eight pounds of steaming cheesy goodness sailed on through the window, scorching the attackers and Pollocking the wall around the window with red sauce.

"That's it, throw snacks at them, that'll slow them up," shouted Tuck. "Fire a salvo of garlic bread next!"

Gabe regained his feet and jumped right up in Theo's face, or he would have if he had been a foot or so taller. "I was trying to save us," he said sternly to Theo's sternum.

Before Theo could answer, Ignacio Nuñez and Ben Miller, a tall, ex–track star in his early thirties, called for them to clear the way. The two men were coming to the broken window with another of the buffet tables. Gabe and Theo helped Ben hold the table against the wall while Nacho nailed the table to the wall. "I found some tools in the basement," Nacho said between hammer blows. Animated dead fingernails clawed at the tabletop as they worked.

"I hate cheese!" screamed the corpse, who had enough equipment to still scream. "It binds me up."

The rest of the undead mob began pounding on the walls around them.

"I need to think," Theo said. "I just need a second to think."

Lena was dressing Tucker Case's wounds with gauze and antibiotic ointment from the chapel's first-aid kit. The burns on his legs and torso were superficial, most of the alcohol fire having been put out by the rain before it could penetrate his clothing, and while his leather bomber jacket had protected him somewhat from his dive through the window, there was a deep cut on his forehead and another on his thigh. One of the bullets that Dale had fired through the table had grazed Tuck's ribs, leaving a gash four inches long and a half inch wide.

"That was the bravest thing I've ever seen," Lena said.

"You know, I'm a pilot," said Tuck, like he did this sort of thing every day. "I couldn't let them hurt you."

"Really?" Lena said, pausing for a moment to look into his eyes. "I'm sorry I was—you were—"

"Actually, you probably couldn't tell, but that thing with the table? Just a really badly executed escape attempt."

Tuck winced as she fastened the bandage over his ribs with some tape.

"You're going to need stitches," Lena said. "Any place I missed?"

Tuck held up his right hand—there were tooth marks on the back of it welling up with blood.

"Oh my God!" Lena said.

"You're going to have to cut his head off," said Joshua Barker, who was standing by watching.

"Whose?" Tuck said. "The guy in the Santa suit, right?"

"No, I mean *your* head," said Josh. "They're going to have to cut off your head or you'll turn into one of them."

Most everyone in the chapel had stopped what they were doing and gathered around Tuck and Lena, seemingly grateful for a point of focus. The pounding on the walls had ceased, and with the exception of the occasional rattling of the door handles, there was only the sound of the wind and rain. The Lonesome Christmas crowd was stunned.

"Go away, kid," said Tuck. "This is no time to be a kid."

"What should we use?" asked Mavis Sand. "This okay, kid?" She held a serrated knife that they'd been using to cut garlic bread.

"That is not acceptable," Tuck said.

"If you don't cut his head off," said Joshua, "he'll turn into one of them and let them in."

"What an imagination this kid has," said Tuck, flashing a grin from face to face, looking for an ally. "It's Christmas! Ah, Christmas, the time when all good people go about not decapitating each other."

Theo Crowe came out of the back room, where he'd been looking for something they could use as a weapon. "Phone lines are down. We'll lose power any minute. Is anyone's cell phone working?"

No one answered. They were all looking at Tuck and Lena.

"We're going to cut off his head, Theo," Mavis said, holding out the bread knife, handle first. "Since you're the law, I think you should do it."

"No, no, no, no, no, no," said Tuck. "And further-more, no."

"No," said Lena, in support of her man.

"You guys have something you want to tell me?" Theo said. He took the bread knife from Mavis and shoved it down the back of his belt.

"I think you were onto something with that killer-robot thing," Tuck said.

Lena stood up and put herself between Theo and Tuck. "It was an accident, Theo. I was digging Christmas trees like I do every year and Dale came by drunk and an-gry. I'm not sure how it happened. One minute he was going to shoot me and the next the shovel was sticking out of his neck. Tucker didn't have anything to do with it. He just happened along and was trying to help."

Theo looked at Tuck. "So you buried him with his gun?"

Tuck climbed painfully to his feet and stood behind

Lena. "I was supposed to see this coming? I was supposed to anticipate that he might come back from the grave all angry and brain hungry, so I should hide his gun from him? This is your town, Constable, you explain it. Usually when you bury a body they don't come back and try to eat your brains the next day."

"Brains! Brains! Brains!" chanted the undead from outside the chapel. The pounding on the walls started again.

"Shut up!" screamed Tucker Case, and to everyone's amazement, they did. Tuck grinned at Theo. "So, I fucked up."

"Ya think?" Theo said. "How many?"

"You should cut his head off over the sink," said Joshua Barker. "That way it won't make as big a mess."

Without a word, Theo reached down and picked Josh up by the biceps, then walked over and handed him to his mother, who looked as if she were going into the first stages of shock. Theo touched his finger to Josh's lips in a shush gesture. Theo looked more serious, more intimidating, more in control than anyone had ever seen him. The boy hid his face in his mother's breasts.

Theo turned to Tuck. "How many?" Theo repeated. "I saw maybe thirty, forty?"

"About that," Tuck said. "They're in different states of decay. Some of them just look like there's little more than bone, others look relatively fresh, and pretty well preserved. None of them seems particularly fast or strong. Dale maybe, some of the fresher ones. It's like they're learning to walk again or something."

There was a loud snap from outside and everyone jumped—one woman literally leaping into a man's arms with a shriek. They all fell into a crouch, listening to a tree falling through branches, expecting the trunk to come crashing through the ceiling beams. The lights went out and the whole church shook with the impact of the big pine hitting the forest floor.

Without missing a beat, Theo snapped on a flashlight he'd had in his back pocket in anticipation of a power outage. Small emergency lamps ignited above the front door, casting everyone in a deep-shadowed directional light.

"Those should last about an hour," Theo said. "There should be some flashlights in the basement, too. Go on. What else did you see, Tuck?"

"Well, they're pissed off and they're hungry. I was kind of busy trying not to get my brains eaten. They seemed pretty adamant about the brain-eating thing. Then they're going to IKEA, I guess."

"This is ridiculous," said Val Riordan, the elegantly coiffed psychiatrist, speaking up for the first time since the whole thing had started. "There's no such thing as a zombie. I don't know what you think is happening here, but you don't have a crowd of brain-eating zombies."

"I'd have to agree with Val," Gabe Fenton said, stepping up beside her. "There's no scientific basis for zombieism—except for some experiments in the Caribbean with blowfish toxins that put people in a state of *near death* with almost imperceptible respiration and pulse, but there was no actual, you know, raising of the dead."

"Yeah?" said Theo, giving them an eloquent deadpan stare. "Brains!" he shouted.

"Brains! Brains! Brains!" came the responding chant from outside; the pounding on the walls resumed.

"Shut up!" Tuck shouted. The dead did.

Theo looked at Val and Gabe and raised an eyebrow. *Well?*

"Okay," Gabe said. "We may need more data."

"No, this can't be happening," said Valerie Riordan. "This is impossible."

"Dr. Val," Theo said. "We know what's happening here. We don't know why, and we don't know how, but we haven't lived in a vacuum all our lives, have we? In this case, denial ain't just a river in Egypt, denial will kill you."

Just then a brick came crashing through one of the windows and thumped into the middle of the chapel floor. Two clawlike hands caught the window ledge and a beat-up male face appeared at the window. The zombie pulled up enough so that he could hook one elbow inside the window, then shouted: "Val Riordan went down on the pimply kid who bags groceries at the Thrifty-Mart!"

A second later, Ben Miller picked up the brick and hurled it back through the window, taking out the zombie face with a sickening squish.

As Ben and Theo lifted the last of the buffet tables into place to be nailed over the window, Gabe Fenton stepped away from Valerie Riordan and looked at her like she'd been dipped in radioactive marmot spittle. "You said you were allergic!"

"We were almost broken up at the time," said Val.

"Almost! Almost! I have third-degree electrical burns on my scrotum because of you!"

Across the room, into Lena Marquez's ear, Tucker Case whispered, "I don't feel so bad about hiding the body now, how 'bout you?" She turned and kissed him hard enough to make him forget for a second that he'd just been shot, set on fire, beaten up, and bitten.

For years the dead had listened, and the dead knew. They knew who was cheating with whom, who was stealing what, and where the bodies were hidden, as it were. Besides the passive listening—those sneaking out for a smoke, sideline conversations at funerals, the walking and talking in the woods, and the sex and scare-yourself activities some of the living indulged in in the graveyard—

there were also those among the living who used a tombstone as some sort of confessional, sharing their deepest secrets with someone who they thought could never talk, saying things they could never say in life.

There were some things that people thought no one else, the living or the dead, could possibly know, but they did.

"Gabe Fenton watches squirrel porn!" screeched Bess Leander, her dead cheek pressed against the wet clapboard siding of the chapel.

"That is not porn, that's my work," Gabe explained to his fellow partyers.

"He doesn't wear pants! Squirrels, doing it, in slow motion. Pantsless."

"Just that one time. Besides, you have to watch in slow motion," Gabe said. "They're squirrels." Everyone turned their flashlights on something else, like they really weren't looking at Gabe.

"Ignacio Nuñez voted for Carter," came a call from outside. The staunch Republican nursery owner was caught like a deer in the flashlights as everyone looked at him. "I was only in this country a year. I'd just become a citizen. I didn't even speak English very well. He said he wanted to help the poor. I was poor."

Theo Crowe reached over and patted Nacho's shoulder.

"Ben Miller used steroids in high school. His gonads are the size of BBs!"

"That is *not* true," exclaimed the track star. "My testicles are perfectly normal size."

"Yeah, if you were seven inches tall," said Marty in the Morning, all dead, all the time.

Ben turned to Theo. "We've got to do something about this."

The others in the room were looking from one to the other, each with a look on his or her face that was much more horrified than when they'd been only facing the prospect of an undead mob eating their brains. These zombies had secrets.

"Theo Crowe's wife thinks she's some kind of warrior mutant killer!" shouted a rotted woman who had once been a psych nurse at the county hospital.

Everybody in the chapel sort of looked at one another and nodded, shrugged, let out a sigh of relief.

"We knew that," yelled Mavis. "Everybody knows that. That's not news."

"Oh, sorry," said the dead nurse. There was a pause; then, "Okay, then. Wally Beerbinder is addicted to painkillers."

"Wally's not here," said Mavis. "He's spending Christmas with his daughter in L.A."

"I got nothing," said the nurse. "Someone else go."

"Tucker Case thinks his bat can talk," shouted Arthur Tannbeau, the dead citrus farmer.

"Who wants to sing Christmas carols?" said Tuck. "I'll start. *'Deck the halls . . . '*"

And so they sang, loud enough to drown out the secrets of the undead. They sang with great Christmas spirit, loud and off-key, until the battering ram hit the front doors.

Chapter 18

YOUR PUNY WORM GOD WEAPONS ARE USELESS AGAINST MY SUPERIOR CHRISTMAS KUNG FU

Molly slipped out the back door of the cabin and around the outside wall until she could see the tall figure standing before her picture window. The fallen wires had stopped sparking out by the street and the stars and moon barely cut through the darkness at all. Strangely enough, she could clearly see the man by her front window because there was a faint glow shining around him.

Radioactive, Molly thought. He wore the long black duster favored by sand pirates. Why, though, would a desert marauder be out in a rainstorm?

She assumed the *Hasso No Kamae* stance, back straight, the sword held high and tilted back over her right shoulder, the sword guard at mouth level, her left foot forward. She was three steps from delivering a deathblow to the intruder. The sword balanced perfectly in her grip, so perfectly that it seemed to weigh nothing at all. She could feel the wet pine needles under her bare feet and wished that she'd put on shoes before dashing out into the night. The cold rain against her bare skin made her think that maybe a sweater would have been a good idea as well.

The glowing man looked toward the opposite corner of the cabin and Molly made her move. Three soft steps and she stood behind him; the edge of her blade lay across the side of his neck. A quick pull and she would cut him to his vertebrae.

"Move and die," Molly said.

"Nuh-uh," said the glowing man.

The tip of Molly's sword extended a foot beyond the stranger's face. He looked at the blade. "I like your sword. Want to see mine?"

"You move, you die," Molly said, thinking that it wasn't the sort of thing you should have to repeat. "Who are you?"

"I'm Raziel," said Raziel. "It's not the sword of the Lord, or anything. Not for destroying cities, just for fighting one or two enemies at a time, or slicing cold cuts. Do you like salami?"

Molly didn't quite know how to proceed. This glowing sand pirate seemed perfectly unafraid, perfectly unconcerned, in fact, that she was holding a razor-sharp blade against his carotid artery. "Why are you looking in my window in the middle of the night?"

"Because I can't see through the wooden part."

Molly snapped her wrists back and smacked Raziel in the side of the head with the flat of her blade.

"Ouch."

"Who are you and why are you here?" Molly said. She snapped her blade back to threaten another smack, and in that instant Raziel stepped away from her, spun, and drew a sword from the middle of his back.

Molly hesitated, just a second, then approached and snapped her blade down, this time in a real attack aimed at his shoulder. Raziel parried the blow and riposted. Molly swept his blade aside and came around with her blade for a cut to the left arm. Raziel got his sword around just in time to deflect her blade down his arm instead of across it. The razor-sharp *tashi* took a long swath of fabric from his coat, as well as a thin slice of flesh down his forearm.

"Hey," he said, looking at his now-flapping sleeve.

There was no blood. Just a dark stripe where the flesh was gone. He started hacking, his sword describing an infinity pattern in the air before him as he drove Molly back through the pine forest toward the road. She quickstepped back, parrying some blows, dodging others, stepping around trees, kicking up wet pine straw as she moved. She could only see her glowing attacker, his sword shining now as well, the darkness around her so complete that she moved only by memory and feel. As she deflected one of the blows, her heel caught on a root and she lost her balance. She started to go over backward and spun as if to catch herself. Raziel's momentum carried him forward, his sword swinging for a target that a second before had been two feet higher, and he ran right onto Molly's blade. She was bent over forward; the blade extended back across her rib cage and through Raziel, extending another two feet out his back. They were frozen there for a moment—him bent over her back, stuck together with her sword—like two dogs who needed a bucket of water thrown on them.

From a crouch, Molly yanked the blade out, then spun, ready to deliver a coup de grâce that would cut her enemy from collarbone to hip.

"Ouch," said Raziel, looking at the hole in his solar plexus. He threw his sword on the ground and prodded the wound with his fingers. "Ouch," he said again, looking up at Molly. "You don't thrust with that kind of sword. You're not supposed to thrust with that kind of sword. No fair."

"You're supposed to die now," Molly said.

"Nuh-uh," said Raziel.

"You can't say nuh-uh to death. That's sloppy debating."

"You poked me with your sword, and cut my coat." He held up his damaged arm.

"Well, you came creeping around here in the middle of the night looking in my windows, and you pulled a sword on me."

"I was just showing it to you. I don't even like it. I want to get web slingers for my next mission."

"Mission? What mission? Did Nigoth send you? He is no longer my higher power, by the way. This is not the kind of support I need."

"Fear not," said Raziel, "for I am a messenger of the Lord, come to bring a miracle for the Nativity."

"You're what?"

"Fear not!"

"I'm not afraid, you nitwit, I just kicked your ass. Are you telling me you're an angel?"

"Come to bring Christmas joy to the child."

"You're a Christmas angel?"

"I bring tidings of great joy, which shall be to all men. Well, not really. This time it's just to one boy, but I memorized that speech, so I like to use it."

Molly let her guard down, the tip of her sword pointed at the ground now. "So the glowing stuff on you?"

"Glory of the Lord," said the angel.

"Oh piss," said Molly. She slapped herself in the forehead. "And I killed you."

"Nuh-uh."

"Don't start with the *nuh-uh* again. Should I call an ambulance or a priest or something?"

"I'm healing." He held up his forearm and Molly watched as the faintly glowing skin expanded to cover the wound.

"Why in the hell are you here?"

"I have a mission—"

"Not here on Earth, here at my house."

"We're attracted to lunatics."

Molly's first instinct was to take his head, but on second thought, she *was* standing in the middle of a pine forest, in freezing rain and gale-force winds, naked, holding a sword, and talking to an angel, so he wasn't exactly announcing the Advent. She *was* a lunatic.

"You want to come inside?" she said.

"Do you have hot chocolate?"

"With minimarshmallows," said the Warrior Babe.

"Blessed are the minimarshmallows," the angel said, swooning a little.

"Come on, then," Molly said as she walked away muttering, "I can't believe I killed a Christmas angel."

"Yep, you screwed the pooch on this one," said the Narrator.

"Nuh-uh," said the angel.

"Get that piano against the door!" Theo yelled.

The bolts on the front door had completely splintered away, and the Masonite buffet table was flexing under the blows of whatever the undead were using for a battering ram. The entire chapel shook with each impact.

Robert and Jenny Masterson, who owned Brine's Bait, Tackle, and Fine Wines, started rolling the upright piano from its spot by the Christmas tree. Both had been through some harrowing moments in Pine Cove's history, and they tended to keep their heads in an emergency.

"Anyone know how to lock these casters?" Robert called.

"We'll need to brace it just the same," Theo said. He turned to Ben Miller and Nacho Nuñez, who seemed to have teamed up for the battle. "You guys look for more heavy stuff to brace the door."

"Where did they get a battering ram?" Tucker Case asked. He was examining the big rubber coasters on the piano, trying to figure out how to lock them.

"Half the forest has blown down tonight," said Lena. "Monterey pines don't have a taproot. They probably just found one that they could lift."

"Turn it on its back," Tuck said. "Brace it against the table."

The ram hit the doors and they popped open six inches. The table hooked under the heavy brass handles was bending and beginning to split. Three arms came through the opening, half a face, the eye drooling out of a rotted socket.

"Push!" Tuck screamed.

They ran the piano up against the braced table, slamming the doors on the protruding limbs. The battering ram hit again, popping the doors open, driving the men back, and rattling their teeth. The undead arms pulled back from the gap. Tuck and Robert shoved the piano against the door and it shut again. Jenny Masterson threw her back against the piano and looked back at the onlookers, twenty or so people who seemed too stunned or too scared to move.

"Don't just stand there, you useless fucks! Help us brace this. If they get in, they're going to eat your brains, too."

Five men pointed flashlights at each other in a "Me? You? Us?" inspection, then shrugged and ran to help push the piano.

"Nice pep talk," said Tuck, his sneakers squeaking on the pine floor as he pushed.

"Thanks, I'm good with the public," Jenny said. "Waitress for twenty years."

"Oh yeah, you waited on us at H.P.'s. Lena, it's our waitress from the other night."

"Nice to see you again, Jenny," said Lena, just as the battering ram hit the door again, knocking her to the floor. "I haven't seen you at yoga class . . ."

"Clear the way, clear the way, clear the way!" called Theo. He and Nacho Nuñez were coming across the floor from the back room carrying an eight-foot-long oak pew. Behind them, Ben Miller was wrestling a pew across the floor by himself. Several of the men who were holding the barricade broke ranks to help him.

"Cantilever these against the piano and nail them to the floor," Theo said.

The heavy benches went up on a diagonal against the back of the piano and Nacho Nuñez toenailed them to the floor.

The benches flexed a little with each blow of the battering ram, but they held fast. After a few seconds, the pounding stopped. Again, there was only the noise of the wind and the rain. Everyone played flashlights around the room, waiting for whatever would come next.

Then they heard Dale Pearson's voice at the side of the chapel. "This way. Bring it this way."

"Back door," someone shouted. "They're carrying it around to the back door."

"More pews," Theo yelled. "Nail them up in the back. Hurry, that door's not as heavy as the front, it won't take two hits like that."

"Can't they just come through one of the walls?" asked Val Riordan, who was trying to join in the effort to hold the line, despite the handicap of her five-hundred-dollar shoes.

"I'm hoping that won't occur to them," Theo said.

Supervising the undead was worse than dealing with a construction crew full of drunks and cokeheads. At least his living crews had all of their limbs and most of their physical coordination. This bunch was pretty floppy. Twenty of the undead were hefting a broken pine-tree trunk a foot thick and as long as a car.

"Move the goddamn tree," Dale growled. "What am I paying you for?"

"Is he paying us?" asked Marty in the Morning, who was hefting at midtree, on a jagged, broken branch. "Are we getting paid?"

"I can't believe you ate all the brains," Warren Talbot, the dead painter, said. "That was supposed to be for everyone."

"Would you shut the fuck up and get the tree around to the back door," Dale yelled, waving his snub-nose revolver.

"The gunpowder gave them a nice peppery flavor," Marty said.

"Don't rub it in," said Bess Leander. "I'm so hungry."

"There will be enough for everyone once we get inside," said Arthur Tannbeau, the citrus farmer.

Dale could tell this wasn't going to work. They were too feeble, they couldn't get enough strength behind the battering ram. The living would be barricading the back door even now.

He pulled some of the more decayed undead off the tree and pushed in those who seemed to have much of their normal strength, but they *were* trying to run up a narrow set of stairs carrying a thousand-pound tree trunk. Even a crew of healthy, living people wouldn't be able to get purchase in this mud. The tree trunk hit the door with an anemic thud. The door flexed just enough to reveal that the living had reinforced it.

"Forget it. Forget it," said Dale. "There are other ways we can get to them. Fan out in the parking lot and start looking for keys in the ignition of people's cars."

"Drive-thru snackage?" said Marty in the Morning. "I like it."

"Something like that," Dale said. "Kid, you with the wax face. You're a motorhead, can you hot-wire a car?"

"Not with only one arm," Jimmy Antalvo slurred. "That dog took my arm."

"It stopped," Lena said. She was checking Tuck's wounds. Blood was seeping through the bandages on his ribs.

Theo turned away from the pilot and looked around the room. The emergency lighting was starting to dim already and his flashlight was panning them like he was looking for suspects. "No one left their keys in their car, did they?"

There were murmurs of denial and heads shaking.

Val Riordan had a perfectly painted eyebrow raised at him. There was a question there, even if it was unspoken.

"Because that's what I'd do," Theo said. "I'd get a car up to speed and crash it right through the wall."

"That would be bad," said Gabe.

"That parking lot had two inches of water and mud the last time I saw it," Tucker Case said. "Not every car is going to get up to speed in that."

"Look, we need to get some help," Theo said. "Someone has to go for help."

"They won't get ten feet," Tuck said. "As soon as you open a door or break a window, they'll be waiting."

"What about the roof?" said Josh Barker.

"Shut up, kid," Tuck said. "There's no way up to the roof."

"Are we going to cut off his head now?" said Josh.

"You have to sever the spinal column or they just keep coming."

"Look," Theo said, playing his flashlight across the center of the ceiling. There was a trapdoor up there, painted over and latched, but it was definitely there.

"It leads to the old bell tower," Gabe Fenton said. "No bell, but it does open onto the roof."

Theo nodded. "From the roof someone could tell where they all were before making his move."

"That hatch is thirty feet up. There's no way to get to it."

Suddenly the high chirp of a barking bat came from above them. A half-dozen flashlights swung around to spotlight Roberto, who was hanging upside down from the star atop the Christmas tree.

"Molly's tree," said Lena.

"It looks sturdy enough," said Gabe Fenton.

"I'll go," said Ben Miller. "I'm still in pretty good shape. If I have to make a run for it, I can."

"Right there, that proves it," said Tuck, an aside to Lena. "No guy with tiny balls would volunteer for that. See how the dead lie."

"I'm driving an old Tercel," Ben said. "I don't think you want me trying to make a run for help in that."

"What we need is a Hummer," said Gabe.

"Yeah, or even a friendly hand job," said Tuck. "But that's later. For now, we need a four-wheel drive."

"You really want to try this?" Theo asked Ben.

The athlete nodded. "I've got the best chance of getting out. Those I can't outrun I'll just go through."

"Okay, then," said Theo. "Let's get that tree over to the middle of the room."

"Not so fast," said Tuck, patting his bandages. "I don't care how fast Micro-nads is, Santa still has two bullets in his gun."

Chapter 19

UP ON THE ROOFTOP,
CLICK, CLICK, CLICK

This is what it's all been about, thought Ben Miller as he climbed into the tiny bell tower atop the chapel. It had taken ten minutes to saw through the painted-closed seams of the hatch with the bread knife, but finally he'd made it, thrown the latch, and crawled from the top of the Christmas tree into the bell tower. There was just enough room to stand, his feet on narrow ledges around the hatch. Thankfully, the bell had been taken away a long time ago. The bell tower was enclosed by louvered vents and the wind whistled through like there was nothing there at all. He was pretty sure he could kick through the vents, hundred-year-old wood, after all, then make his way across the steep roof, drop off whichever side looked safe, and make it to the parking lot and the red Explorer he was holding the keys for. Thirty miles south to the highway-patrol post and help would be on the way.

All of the years after high school and college when he had continued to train, all the hours of roadwork, all the weights and swimming and high-protein diets, it all came down to this moment. Keeping himself in shape all these years when no one really seemed to care would finally pay off. Anything out there that he couldn't out-run, he could take out with a lowered shoulder. (He'd played one season as a jay-vee halfback in addition to his varsity track career.)

"You okay, Ben?" Theo yelled from below.

"Yeah. I'm ready."

He took a deep breath, braced his back against one side of the bell tower, then kicked at the louvered slats on the opposite side. They broke away on the first kick and he was nearly launched out on the roof feetfirst. He fought to get his balance—turned around on his stomach and scooted backward out the opening onto the roof. Facedown, he was looking down the length of the Christmas tree at a dozen hopeful faces below.

"Hold tight. I'll be back soon with help," he said. Then he pushed back until he was on his hands and knees on the peak of the roof, cold wetness cutting everywhere he touched.

"Please, bitch," came a voice from right by Ben's ear. He jumped sideways, and started to slide down the roof. Something caught his sweater, pulling him back, then something hard and cold was pressed against his forehead.

The last thing he heard was Santa saying, "Pretty fucking tricky for a jock."

Below, in the chapel, they heard the gunshot.

Dale Pearson held the dead track star by the back of the collar, thinking, *Eat now, or save it for after the massacre?* Below him on the ground, the rest of the undead were begging for treats. Warren Talbot, the landscape painter, had made his way halfway up the pine-tree trunk that Dale had used to climb up on the roof.

"Please, please, please, please," said Warren. "I'm so hungry."

Dale shrugged and let go of Ben Miller's collar, then gave the body a shove with his boot, sending it sliding down the roof and off the side to the hungry mob. Warren looked behind him at where the body had fallen, then at Dale.

"You bastard. Now I'll never get any."

Disgusting sucking sounds were rising from below.

"Yeah, well, the quick and the dead, Warren. The quick and the dead."

The dead painter slid back down his tree and out of sight.

Dale had some revenge to take. He stuck his head inside the bell tower and looked down at the horrified faces below. The wiry little biologist was climbing up the Christmas tree toward the open hatch.

"Come on up," screamed Dale. "We haven't even gotten to the main course."

Dale spotted his ex-wife, Lena, staring up, and the blond guy who had charged them with the buffet table had his arm around her.

"Die, slut!" Dale let go of the edge of the bell tower and aimed the .38 down the Christmas tree at Lena. He saw her eyes go wide, then something hit him in the face, something furry and sharp. Claws cut into his cheeks and scratched at his eyes. He grabbed for his attacker and in doing so lost his balance and fell backward. He slid down the side of the roof and off the edge onto his feasting minions.

"Roberto!" Tuck yelled. "Get back in here."

"He's gone," said Theo. "He's outside."

Tuck started to climb up the Christmas tree behind Gabe. "I'll get him. Let me come up and call him."

Theo grabbed the pilot around the waist and pulled him back. "Close and lock the hatch, Gabe."

"No," Tuck said.

Gabe Fenton looked down briefly, then his eyes went wide when he realized how high above the floor he was. He quickly pushed the bell-tower hatch shut and latched it.

"He'll be okay," said Lena. "He got away."

Gabe Fenton backed down the Christmas tree. When he got to the lower branches, he felt some hands at his waist, steadying him down the last few steps. When he hit the floor, he turned around into Valerie Riordan's arms. He pushed away so as not to smudge her makeup. She pulled him out of the branches of the tree.

"Gabe," she said. "You know when I said you weren't engaged in the real world?"

"Yeah."

"I'm sorry."

"Okay."

"I just wanted you to know that. In case our brains are eaten by zombies without me having a chance to say it."

"That means a lot to me, Val. Can I kiss you?"

"No, sweetheart, I left my purse in the car and don't

have any lipstick to touch up. But we can knock out one last stand-up quickie in the basement before we die if you'd like." She smiled.

"What about the kid at the Thrifty-Mart?"

"Squirrel porn?" She raised a perfectly drawn eyebrow.

He took her by the hand. "Yes, I think I'd like that," he said, leading her to the back room and the stairs.

"What's that smell?" Theo Crowe said, remarkably glad to turn his attention away from Gabe and Val. "Anybody smell that? Tell me that's not—"

Skinner was sniffing the air and whimpering.

"What is that?" Nacho Nuñez was following the smell to one of the barricaded windows. "It's coming from over here."

"Gasoline," said Lena.

Chapter 20

WINGING IT

The angel had opened six envelopes of powdered hot-chocolate mix and handpicked out all the minimarshmallows. "They trap them in these little prisons with the brown powder. You must free them to put them in the cup," the angel explained, tearing open another packet, pouring the contents into a bowl, picking up the little marshmallows, and dropping them into his mug.

"Kill him while he's counting the marshmallows," said the Narrator. *"He's a mutant. No angel could be that stupid. Kill him, you crazy bitch, he's the enemy."*

"Nuh-uh," said Raziel, into his marshmallow foam.

Molly looked at him over the rim of her mug. By the candlelight in the kitchen, he certainly was a striking fellow—those sharp features, the lineless face, the hair, and now the chocolate-marshmallow mustache. Not to mention the intermittent glowing in the dark, which had been helpful when she was looking for some matches to light the candles.

"You can hear the voice in my head?" she asked.

"Yes. And in my head."

"I'm not religious," Molly said. Under the table, she held the *tashi* with her free hand, its blade resting across her bare thighs.

"Oh, me either," said the angel.

"I mean, I'm not religious, so why are you here?"

"Lunatics. We're attracted to them. It has something to do with the mechanics of faith. I don't really understand it. Do you have any more?" He held up the empty cocoa envelope. His mug was overflowing with melted marshmallow foam.

"No, that's the whole box. So you're attracted to me because I'm loony and will believe anything?"

"Yes, I think so. And because no one will believe you. So there's no violation of faith."

"Right."

"But you are attractive in other ways, too," added the angel quickly, as if someone had suddenly smacked him in the head with a sock full of people skills. "I like your sword and those."

"My breasts?" It wasn't the first time that someone

had said that sort of thing to her, but it was the first time it had come from a messenger of God.

"Yes. Zoe has those. She's an archangel like me. Well, not like me. She has those."

"Uh-huh. So there are female angels as well?"

"Oh yes. Not always. Everyone was changed after you happened."

"Me?"

"Man. Mankind. Women. You. Before we were all one kind. But then you happened, and we were divided up and given parts. Some got those, others got other things. I don't know why."

"So you have parts?"

"Would you like to see?"

"Wings?" Molly asked. She actually wouldn't mind seeing his wings, if he had them.

"No, we all have those. I mean my special parts. Would you like to see?" He stood and reached down the front of his pants.

It wasn't the first time she'd had an offer like that, but it was the first time it had come from a messenger of God.

"No, that's okay." She grabbed his forearm and guided him back into his seat.

"Okay, then. I should go. I have to check on the miracle and then go home."

"The miracle?"

"A Christmas miracle. That's why I'm here. Oh look, you have a scar on one of them."

"He has the attention span of a hummingbird," the Narrator hissed. *"Put him out of his misery."*

The angel was pointing to the jagged five-inch scar above Molly's right breast, the one she'd gotten when a stunt went wrong while filming *Mechanized Death: Warrior Babe VII*. The injury that had gotten her fired, the scar that had ended her career as a B-movie action heroine.

"Does it hurt?" asked the angel.

"Not anymore," Molly said.

"Can I touch?"

It wasn't the first time that someone had asked, but—well, you know . . . "Okay," she said.

His fingers were long and fine, his fingernails a little too long for a guy, she thought, but his touch was warm and radiated from her breast through her whole body.

When he pulled his hand away, he said, "Better?"

She touched where he had touched. It was smooth. Completely smooth. The scar was gone. The angel blurred in her vision as tears welled up in her eyes.

"You complete shit bag of sentimental saccharine," said the Narrator.

"Thank you," Molly said, with a hint of a sniffle. "I didn't know you could—"

"I'm good with weather," said the angel.

"Idiot!" the Narrator said.

"I have to go now," said Raziel, rising from his chair. "I have to go to the church to see if the miracle has worked."

Molly led him through the living room to the front door. She held the door for him. Even so, the wind whipped his coat around him and she could see the white tips of his wings below. She smiled, laughing and crying at the same time.

"Bye," the angel said. He walked away into the woods.

As Molly closed the door, something dark flew through it. The candles in the living room had blown out, so all she could see was a shadow flying through the house, disappearing into the kitchen.

She got the door shut and trod into the kitchen, holding her sword at a low ready. By the candlelight in the kitchen, she could see the shadow over the kitchen window, two eyes shining orange back there in the dark.

She picked up a candle from the table and moved toward the window until the shadow cast shadows of its own. It was some kind of animal, hanging from the shutter over the sink, looking like a black towel with a little doggy face. It didn't seem dangerous, just, well, a little goofy.

"Well, this is it. I am getting back on my meds tomorrow, if I have to borrow the money from Lena."

"Not so fast," said the Narrator. *"It'll be so lonely in here when I'm gone. And you'll be back to wearing your normal clothes. Jeans and sweaters, you can't want that."*

Ignoring the Narrator, Molly approached the creature on the shutters until she was only two feet away and staring right into its eyes. "Angels are one thing, but I don't even know what in the hell you are, little guy."

"Fruit bat," said Roberto.

"He might be a Spaniard," said the Narrator. *"Did you hear the accent?"*

"I'm going out there," Theo Crowe said, finding a grip on the Christmas tree.

"He still has one bullet," said Tucker Case.

"They are going to torch the place. I've got to get out there."

"To do what? You going to take their matches away?"

Lena took Theo by the arm. "Theo, they'll never get a fire started in this rain and wind. Don't go out there. Ben didn't make it two steps."

"If I can get to an SUV, I can start running over people," Theo said. "Val gave me the keys to her Range Rover."

"Well, that's not going to work," said Tuck. "There's a bunch of them. You might get some of the feeble ones, but the rest will just run into the woods where you can't get to them."

"Fine. Suggestions? This place will burn like tinder, rain or no rain. If I don't do something we're going to get roasted."

Lena looked at Tuck. "Maybe Theo's right. If he can drive them into the woods, maybe the rest of us can make a break for the parking lot. They can't get all of us."

"Fine," Theo said. "Divide people up into groups of five and six. Give the strongest member of each group the key to an SUV. Make sure everyone knows where they're going once they get out the door. When you hear the horn on the Range Rover play 'Shave and a Haircut,' it will mean I've done what I can do. Everyone make a break for it."

"Wow, you came up with that while stoned," Tuck said. "I'm impressed."

"Just get everyone ready. I'm not going out on that roof until I'm sure no one is waiting for me."

"What if we hear a gunshot? What if they get you before you get to the car?"

Theo pulled a key out of his pocket and handed it to Tuck. "Then it would be your turn, wouldn't it? Val had her spare car key with her, too."

"Wait a minute. I'm not running out there. You have an excuse, you're stoned, you're a cop, your wife threw you out, and your life is in shreds. Things are going good for me."

"When Constable Crowe leaves, then can we cut off his head?" asked Joshua Barker.

"Okay, maybe not," said Tuck.

"I'm going," Theo said. "Get everyone ready at the door."

The lanky constable made his way up the Christmas tree. Tuck watched him climb out on the roof, then turned to the others. "Okay, you guys heard him. Let's break into groups of five and six by the front doors. Nacho, grab the hammer, we're going to have to pull the nails on the reinforcements. Who's driving an SUV?"

Everyone but the children raised their hands.

"It won't spark, it's wet," said Marty in the Morning. He was trying to coax fire out of a drenched disposable lighter. The undead stood around him, looking at the pile of gasoline-sodden debris they'd piled against the side of the chapel.

"I love barbecue," said Arthur Tannbeau. "Every Sunday out at the ranch, we used to—"

"Only in California could one refer to a citrus farm as a ranch," interrupted Malcolm Cowley. "As if you and the yahoos would all go out on horseback to round up the tangerines."

"Didn't anyone find a dry lighter or matches in any of the cars?" Dale Pearson said.

"No one smokes anymore," said Bess Leander. "Disgusting filthy habit anyway."

"Said the woman who still has brain matter on her chin from that fellow in the sweater," said Malcolm.

Bess smiled coyly, most of her gums visible through her receded lips. "They were so tasty—it was like he'd never used them."

There was a chirp from the front of the chapel and all of them looked. Yellow lights flashed on one of the vehicles up there.

"Someone's making a break for it," screamed Dale. "I thought I told you to keep an eye on the roof."

"I did," said the one-armed Jimmy Antalvo. "It's dark. I can't see shit."

As they rushed down the side of the chapel toward the front, they saw a dark shadow slide off the side of the roof to the ground.

Chapter 21

AVENGING ANGEL

Oh shit, oh shit, oh shit, oh shit, Theo thought. He twisted his ankle when he hit the ground; pain shot up his leg like liquid fire. He fell and rolled onto his back in the mud. He'd pushed the remote button that unlocked the Range Rover too soon. The vehicle had chirped and the lights had blinked, alerting the undead. He'd made the jump blind, and missed. They were coming for him.

He pushed himself up and started hopping toward the Range Rover, the car key ready in his right hand, his flashlight lost behind him in the mud.

"Grab him, you rotting fucks," screamed Dale Pearson.

Theo fell forward as his good foot slipped out from

under him, but he rolled back to his feet, a bolt of pain shooting white-hot across his shin. He caught himself on the back window of the black Range Rover, snatching at the rear wiper for balance. He risked a glance back toward his pursuers and heard a loud thump by his head followed by a deafening screech. He turned just in time to see a skeletal woman sliding across the roof of the Range Rover, leading with her teeth. He ducked, but not before he felt fingernails raking his neck, teeth thumping into his scalp. She rode him to the ground and he could feel a grating pain in his head as the zombie tried to bite through his skull. His face was pushed into the mud. His nostrils and mouth filled with water, and amid a flashing whiteness of terror he thought, *I'm so sorry, Molly.*

"Yuck! That's hideous!" said Bess Leander, spitting a couple of teeth on the back of Theo's head.

Marty in the Morning grabbed Theo by the head and licked the teeth marks that Bess had left. "That's horrible. He's stoned. I'm not eating stoned brains."

The undead moaned in disappointment.

"Get him up," said Dale.

Theo inhaled a great spray of mud along with his first breath and he went into a coughing fit as the undead lifted him up and held him against the back window of the Range Rover. Someone wiped the mud out of his eyes, and a stench that made him gag filled his nostrils. He could see the dead but animated face of Dale Pearson only inches from his own. The corpse's foul breath overwhelmed him. Theo tried to twist away from the evil Santa, but decaying hands held his head fast.

"Hey, hippie," said Dale. He held Theo's flashlight down by his Santa beard to illuminate his face from below. There were two stripes of bloody drool running down either side of the beard. "You're not thinking that your pot-smoking ways are going to save you, are you? Don't." He pulled a snub-nose revolver out of the pocket of his red coat and shoved it under Theo's chin. "We'll have plenty to eat. We can afford to waste you."

Dale ripped open the Velcro fasteners of Theo's jacket and started feeling around his waist. "No gun? You suck as a lawman, hippie." He went to the pockets of Theo's cop shirt. "But this! The one thing you can be depended on for."

Dale held up Theo's lighter, then reached in, tore the whole pocket off the cop shirt, and wrapped the dry fabric around the lighter. "Marty, try this. Keep it dry." Dale gave the lighter to a rotting guy with a wet Ziggy Stardust red mullet, who slogged back to the pile of debris at the side of the chapel.

Theo watched as Marty in the Morning bent over the pile of plywood, pine branches, two-by-fours, cardboard, and the torn-up body of Ben Miller. The wind was still whipping, the rain less intense now, but even so the drops stung Theo's face when they hit.

Don't light, don't light, don't light, Theo chanted in his head, but then his hope drained away when he saw the orange flame catch on the debris, and Marty in the Morning pull away with his sleeve on fire.

Dale Pearson stepped aside so Theo could see the fire whipping up the side of the building, then put the .38 against Theo's temple. "Take a good look at our little barbecue fire, hippie. It's the last thing you're going to see. We're gonna eat your crazy wife's brains charbroiled."

Theo smiled, happy that Molly wasn't inside, wouldn't be part of the massacre.

"I didn't hear 'Shave and a Haircut,'" said Ignacio Nuñez. "Did you hear 'Shave and a Haircut'?"

Tuck panned his flashlight across a dozen frightened faces, then one whole side of the chapel went orange with the light from the fire outside the windows. One woman screamed, others stared in horror as smoke started to snake in around the window frames.

"Change of plan," Tuck said. "We go now. Guys in front of your groups. Give the car keys to the next person back."

"They'll be waiting for us," said Val Riordan.

"Fine, you burn up," Tuck said. "Guys, knock over whatever gets in your way, everyone behind just keep going for the cars."

All the barricades and braces had been removed from the chapel doors. Tuck put his shoulder against one door, Gabe Fenton was on the other. "Ready. One, two, three!"

They threw their shoulders against the doors and bounced back into the others. The doors had only opened a couple of inches. Someone shone a flashlight through the gap to reveal a huge pine-tree trunk braced against one of the doors.

"New plan," shouted Tuck.

Theo tried to look at the fire, but he couldn't see beyond the undead eyes of Dale Pearson. Thought had fled. There was just fear and anger and the pressure of the gun barrel against his temple.

He heard a whooshing sound and a thump by his ear and the gun barrel was gone. Dale Pearson was stepping away from him, holding a dark stump where his gun hand had just been. Dale opened his mouth to shout something, but in that second a thin line appeared across his face at nostril level and half of his head slid to the ground. He slumped in a pile at Theo's feet. The hands that were holding Theo let go.

"Brains!" screamed one of the undead. "Crazy-woman brains!"

Theo fell on top of Dale's rekilled body, then spun around to see what was happening.

"Hi, honey," Molly said. She stood on the roof of the Range Rover, grinning, wearing a leather jacket, sweatpants, and her red Converse All Stars, holding the ancient Japanese sword in *Hasso No Kamae* before her, the blade gleaming orange in the light from the burning church. There was a dark swath across the blade where it had hewn the head of the zombie Santa. Theo had never been a religious man, but he thought in that instant that this must be what it was like to look on the face of an avenging angel.

The zombies who had been holding Theo reached for Molly's legs, and in a single motion she stepped back and brought the sword around in a low arc that sent a rain of severed hands flying into the mud. The undead wailed around her, and tried to claw their way onto the SUV with their stumps. Bess Leander tried to replicate the move she had used on Theo, stepping up on the hood behind Molly and diving across the roof of the Range Rover. Molly spun and sidestepped, making a low swing with her sword that would have not looked out of place on a golf course. Bess's head rolled off the top of the Land Rover into Theo's lap. He pushed it aside and got to his feet.

"Honey, you might want to go let everyone out of the chapel before they burn up," said Molly. "I'm not sure you want to watch this."

" 'Kay," said Theo.

The undead had left their stations at the front and back doors of the chapel, where they had been waiting to ambush the escaping partyers, and charged Molly. Three fell headless while Molly stood on the Land Rover, but as they surrounded her, she ran and leaped over the heads of the mob, landing behind them.

Theo ran for the front doors of the chapel, his vision blurred from the rain and the blood running into his eyes from the bite wound on his head. He looked back for a second and saw Molly sailing over the top of her attackers.

He nearly ran into two great pine logs that had been braced against the chapel doors. He looked back a second and caught a glimpse of Molly mowing down two more zombies, one split down the middle from the crown of his head to his sternum, then he turned and tried to get his back under one of the logs.

"Theo, is that you?" Gabe Fenton had his face pressed in an inch-wide gap between the doors.

"Yeah. There are logs against the doors," Theo said. "I'm going to try to move them."

Theo took three deep breaths and lifted for all he was worth, feeling as if veins would explode in his temples. The wound on his head throbbed with every heartbeat.

But the tree trunk moved a couple of inches. He could do this.

"Is it working?" yelled Gabe.

"Yeah, yeah," said Theo. "Give me a second."

"It's filling up with smoke in here, Theo."

"Right." Theo strained again and the log moved another two inches to the right. Another foot and they'd be able to get the door open.

"Hurry, Theo," said Jenny Masterson. "It's—" She went into a coughing fit and couldn't finish what she was saying. Theo could hear everyone coughing inside. Wails of rage and pain were coming from the side of the chapel where Molly was fighting. She must be okay, they were still yelling about eating her brain.

Another lift, another two inches. Gray smoke was streaming out the crack between the doors. Theo fell to his knees with the effort and almost passed out. He shook himself back into consciousness, and as he prepared to put his back into another effort, hoping it wouldn't be his last, he noticed that the screaming had stopped at the side of the chapel. Rain, wind, the coughing of the trapped, and the crackle of the fire. That was all he heard.

"Oh my God. Molly!" he screamed.

A hand on his cheek, a voice at his ear. "Hey, sailor, need a little hand getting your church door open, if you know what I mean?"

Sirens sounded in the distance. Someone had seen the burning chapel through the storm and had somehow gotten through to the volunteer fire department. The Lonesome Christmas survivors were gathered in the middle of the parking lot, illuminated by headlights. The heat from the fire had driven them nearly seventy-five yards to the street.

Even this far away, Theo could feel the heat on his cheek from the fire as Lena Marquez bandaged his head. Others sat in the open hatchbacks of SUVs, trying to catch their breath after being exposed to the smoke, drinking bottled water or just lying there dazed.

Around the burning chapel the wet pine forest steamed, a great white cloud rising into the sky. Down the left side of the chapel: carnage—a rekilling ground of the undead, where Molly had hacked them into sub-mission, even chasing down the last few in the woods and decapitating them after she and Theo had let the partyers out of the chapel.

Molly sat beside Theo, under the open hatchback of someone's Expedition.

"How did you know?" he asked. "How could you possibly have known?"

"The bat told me," Molly said.

"You mean he showed up and you said, 'What's wrong, boy, is Timmy trapped down a well?,' and he barked to tell you that's what was wrong? Like that?"

"No," Molly said. "It was like, 'Your husband and a bunch of other people have barricaded themselves in the chapel against a horde of brain-eating zombies and you need to go save them.' Like that. He has some kind of accent. Sounds Spanish."

"I for one am glad that you went off your meds," said Tucker Case, who was standing next to Lena as she bandaged Theo's head. "A few hallucinations are a small price to pay, if you ask me."

Molly held up her hand for him to be quiet. She stood and brushed the pilot aside, looking back toward the burning church. A tall dark figure in a long coat was coming toward them through the killing field.

"Oh no," said Theo. "Everyone get in the cars and lock them."

"No," Molly said, dismissing Theo's instructions

with a distracted backward wave. "We're okay." She met
the angel in the middle of the parking lot.

"Merry Christmas," said the angel.

"Yeah, you, too," said Molly.

"Have you seen the child? Joshua?" asked Raziel.

"There's a kid over there with the others," said
Molly. "That's probably him."

"Take me to him."

"That's him," Theo said. "That's the robot guy."

"Shhhhhh," Molly shushed.

Raziel walked to where Emily Barker was holding
her son, Joshua, sitting on the back of Molly's Honda.

"Mom," wailed Joshua. He hid his face in his
mother's chest.

But Emily was still stunned by witnessing her mate's
death, and she didn't react at all except to hold the boy
tighter.

Raziel put his hand on the boy's head. "Fear not,"
he said. "For I bring you tidings of great joy. Behold,
your Christmas wish has been granted." The angel
waved toward the fire and the carnage and the exhausted and terrified survivors as if he were a game-
show hostess presenting a washer/dryer set. "Not what
I would have wished for," the angel said, "but I am but
a lowly messenger."

Josh rolled in his mother's arms and faced the angel. "I didn't ask for this. This isn't what I wished for."

"Sure it is," said Raziel. "You wished that the Santa you saw killed be brought back to life."

"No, I didn't."

"That's what you said. You said you wanted him brought back to life."

"That's not what I meant," said Joshua. "I'm a kid. I don't always get stuff right."

"I'll vouch for that," said Tucker Case, stepping up behind the angel. "He *is* a kid, and he is wrong most of the time."

"We still should cut your head off," said Josh.

"See," said Tuck. "Always wrong."

"Well, if you didn't mean you wanted him brought back to life, what did you mean?" asked Raziel.

"I didn't mean I wanted Santa to be a zombie and kill big, dumb Brian and everything. I wanted everything to be okay. Like it never happened. So it would be a good Christmas."

"That's not what you said," said Raziel.

"That's what I wanted," said Joshua.

"Oh," said the angel. "Sorry."

"So he's an angel?" Theo said to Molly. "Like a real angel?"

Molly nodded, smiling.

"Not a killer robot?"

Molly shook her head. "He's here to grant a Christmas wish, to one child."

"Like it never happened?" the angel asked Joshua.

"Yeah!" said Josh.

"Oops," said the angel.

Molly stepped over and put her hand on the angel's shoulder. "Raziel, you fucked up. Fix it?"

The angel looked at her and grinned. Perfect teeth, if a little sharp.

"So be it," he said. "Glory to God in the highest, peace on Earth, goodwill toward men."

Chapter 22

A PERFECT LONESOME CHRISTMAS

The archangel Raziel hovered outside the Santa Rosa Chapel's big cathedral window, looking through a small pane of pink glass that formed Saint Rosa's cheek. He smiled at his handiwork, then beat his great wings and flew off to find some chocolate to sustain him on his trip home.

Life is messy. Would that every puzzle piece fell into place, every word was kind, every accident happy, but such is not the case. Life is messy. People, generally, suck. This year, however, the Lonesome Christmas party in Pine Cove was coming off with clarified joy, an infectious goodwill, and a general harmony of spirit that shone in the guests with a smooth, high polish—a no-mess affair.

"Theo," Molly said, "can you grab the other lasagna pans out of the back." She was carrying two of the long stainless-steel pans herself, and she was careful to bend at the knees as she set them down on the buffet table to keep the back of her short cocktail dress in the realm of decency. It was a plunging neckline LBD (little black dress) she'd borrowed from Lena just for the party—the first low-cut thing she'd worn in years.

"We could have barbecued after all," Theo said.

"I told you fucksticks that the storm would turn south," Mavis Sand growled as she sawed the end off a baguette like the *moyl* at a titanic bris. (Some people's goodwill shines differently than others'.)

Molly set down her lasagna and turned around into the arms of her praying mantis of a husband. "Whoa, sailor, Warrior Babe's got work to do."

"I just wanted to tell you," Theo said, "before everyone gets here, that you look absolutely stunning."

Molly brushed her hand across her neckline. "Scars don't do that, do they? They don't just disappear overnight like that, right?"

"Doesn't matter to me," Theo said. "Never mattered. Wait until you see what I got you for Christmas."

Molly kissed him on the chin. "I love you, even if

you have mutant tendencies; now free me, Lena needs help with the salad."

"No, I don't," said Lena, coming out of the back room carrying a huge salad bowl. Tucker Case followed close behind with a stainless caddie of dressings.

"Oh, Theo," Lena said, "I hope you don't mind, but Dale is going to come by in his Santa suit tonight."

"I thought you guys were in combat," Theo said.

"We were, but he surprised me a couple of nights ago when I was stealing some of his Christmas trees, and was just losing his temper when Tucker happened along and popped him in the nose."

Tucker Case grinned. "I'm a pilot, we're used to handling tense situations."

"Anyway," Lena continued, "Dale was drunk. He started crying, getting maudlin, talking about how he was having trouble with his new girlfriend, saying how he hated that everyone saw him as the evil developer, so I invited him here. Thought maybe if he could do something nice for the kids, it would make him feel better."

"No problem," Theo said. "I'm glad you two are getting along."

"Hey, Theo!" yelled Joshua Barker as he ran across the chapel floor toward them. "Mom says Santa will be at the party."

"A quick appearance, Josh, then he has to get on his

route," Theo said. He looked up to see Emily Barker and her boyfriend/husband/whatever Brian Henderson coming across the room. Brian was wearing a red Star Fleet Command shirt.

"Merry Christmas, Theo," Emily said.

Theo hugged Emily and shook Brian's hand.

"Theo, have you seen Gabe Fenton?" Brian asked. "I wanted to show him the shirt, I think he'll get a kick out of it. You know, nerd solidarity."

"He was here a little bit ago, Brian, but then Val Riordan arrived and they were talking. I haven't seen them for a while."

"Maybe they went for a walk. Beautiful evening, isn't it?"

"Isn't it," said Molly, coming to Theo's side.

"He said he was good with weather," said the Narrator.

"Shhhhhhh," said Molly.

"Pardon?" Brian said.

Out behind the chapel, the dead were feeling festive as well.

"He's going to do her right here in the graveyard," said Marty in the Morning. *"Who would have thought a shrink could moan like that. A little carnal scream therapy, huh, doc?"*

"No way," said Bess Leander. *"She's wearing Armani, she's not going to mess up that outfit."*

"You're right," said Jimmy Antalvo. *"They'll just suck*

face and take the party home for makeup sex. But how do you know she's wearing Armani?"

"You know what?" said Bess. *"I have no idea. Just a feeling, I guess."*

"I do hope they sing 'Good King Wenceslas,' " said Esther, the schoolteacher. *"I just love that song."*

"Has anyone seen the biologist's dreadful dog?" asked Malcolm Cowley, the dead book dealer. *"Last year the beast urinated on my headstone three times."*

"He was sniffing around a minute ago," said Marty in the Morning, *"but he went inside when they started to bring the food out."*

Inside, Skinner was sitting under the Christmas tree, looking at the strangest creature he'd ever seen. It was hanging from the lower branches, but it didn't look like a squirrel, or smell like food; in fact, it had a face that looked like another dog. Skinner whimpered and sniffed the air. If it was a dog, where was its butt? How could he say hello if he couldn't sniff its butt? He took a tentative step back to study the thing.

"What are you looking at?" said Roberto.

And Before We Knew It, Christmas Had Rolled Around Again

A year later—a year after the best Lonesome Christmas ever—a stranger drove into town. His name was William Johnson, and he worked in a cubicle inside a great glass cube in Silicon Valley, where he moved thingies around on a screen all day. He lived by himself in a condo off the interstate and every Christmas he took two weeks off and traveled to a small town where no one knew him to practice his own special holiday tradition. This year he had chosen Pine Cove for his little party and he was especially excited because it was the closest to home he'd ever done the deed. He allowed himself to be reckless because this was his twelfth consecutive Christmas trip—an even dozen—and he felt he deserved a treat.

Also, his vacation had been held up for a week by a late push on a project, so he didn't have time to do the research he normally did—he just couldn't afford more travel time.

William had never looked deeply into why he'd chosen Christmas to practice his hobby. It just happened that it had been Christmastime when he'd had his first celebration—a trip to Elko, Nevada, to meet a woman he'd met on a Usenet, and when it turned out that she not only did not live in Elko, but, in fact, was not a she at all, he took his frustrations out on a local truck-stop prostitute and found that he quite liked it. Then again, it could be because his mother (the whore!) had never given him a middle name. You were supposed to have a middle name, dammit. Especially if you were going to be a collector like William.

As he drove the rented cargo van up Cypress Street, he began humming the "Twelve Days of Christmas" to himself, and smiled. Twelve. In a cooler in the back of the van, vacuum-packed between sheets of clear plastic in a single row, lined up across the dry ice like little pink pillows, he kept his eleven human tongues.

He pulled into a space in front of the Head of the Slug Saloon, adjusted his fake mustache, fluffed up the fat suit he wore under his clothes that made him look twenty years older than he was, and stepped out of the van. The rustic, out-of-time, generally run-down look of the

Head of the Slug made it seem like the perfect place to find his twelfth.

"*And a partridge in a pear tree,*" he sang softly to himself.

There had been a meltdown of themes for the Christmas for the Lonesome that year.

"It's fucking Christmas," Mavis had growled. "Tack up some tinsel, cut down a pine tree, throw some rum in the eggnog, and you're good to go. What do you want, the Second Coming?"

In retrospect, everyone felt a little uneasy about that perfect Lonesome Christmas. There had been dreams, nightmares, even flashbacks to things that no one could remember actually happening, and strangely enough, rather than discourage them from attending this year, the revelers were compelled to go, to make it a great party, as if they somehow had to fix something that wasn't broken. People had been talking about it since Halloween, which put a great deal of pressure on the planners.

"How about we do a Mexican Christmas, a *posada*?" Lena Marquez suggested. "I'll make enchiladas, we'll have a piñata, we can get . . ."

"A burro!" Mavis interrupted. "With a dick like a whiffle-ball bat."

"Mavis!" Lena said *adios* to her *posada* as it sank into the cesspool of Mavis's Tijuana sex show imagination.

"A costume party," Molly said, with great gravity, as if she were, indeed, announcing the Second Coming, or perhaps channeling a message from Vigoth the Worm God.

"No," said Theo, who had been sitting down the bar that day and was really trying to stay out of it. "People are weird when they are in costume. I see it all the time at Halloween. It's like a license for them to act like assholes."

The women all looked at Theo, and for the expression they gave him, he might have just squeezed a skunk into their root beers.

"Great idea," said Lena.

"I'm in," said Mavis.

"Everyone loves to put on an outfit," said Molly.

"Yes, you do," said Mavis.

"And she should," said Lena, a little elbow in her friend's ribs.

"I like the outfit you wore last year," said Theo.

And they looked at him.

"Oh hell, what do I know?" said the constable. "Me here with my XY chromosome, I don't know anything."

"Tucker and I stayed in on Halloween," said Lena. "The bat was sick. So this will be a fun opportunity to dress up."

"And I might still be able to put together something with a burro," said Mavis.

"I'm outta here," Theo said, sliding off his stool and heading toward the door.

"Don't be such a fucking pilgrim, Theo," Mavis said. "There's one in the nativity scene down at the Catholic church."

"But they're not doing it," Theo said, not even pausing to look back.

And then he was out the door.

"You don't know what happened after they took the picture they made that from," Mavis called after him, as if that made perfect sense. "There were shepherds, for Christ sakes!"

"I have a Kendra costume I haven't worn since the movie," Molly said. "Full plate armor, only—you know—girly."

"That's Christmassy," Mavis said.

"We could decorate it," Lena said.

"Yeah, Mavis, we can put holly and fake snow on the death spikes," Molly said, miming festive holiday death spikes that would protrude cheerfully from her forearms.

"I want to come as Snow White," Lena said. "Do you think Tucker will wear a Prince Charming costume if I get it for him?"

"No way," Mavis growled. "He's too worried about ruining his image as the nitwit who talks to a fruit bat."

"No one appreciates your sarcasm, Mavis."

"Well, costumes can be optional, as far as I'm concerned, because I'm making fruitcake this year." Mavis winked and her eyelid stuck shut until she gave herself a little thump in the temple. "Special fruitcake."

A middle-aged man in a trucker's hat and generic work clothes had somehow slipped into the bar and onto one of the stools without anyone noticing, but Mavis saw him staring at them when she unstuck her eyelid.

"What can I get you, sweet cheeks?"

"Just a draft," said the stranger.

"Everything alright?" Mavis asked. The guy seemed dazed. Not that she wasn't used to that, but she didn't like it when people were out of it and she didn't get to profit from it.

"Just couldn't be better," said the stranger, tearing his gaze from the back of Lena's neck.

William Johnson felt that he must have been leading a charmed life. Not since the very first time (and there's really no repeating that, is there?) had he been lucky enough to stumble over the "intended" so quickly. She was perfect, just perfect. Delicate and sexy, proud and determined—the kind of woman who wouldn't give him a second look. She hadn't, had she? And that neck and jawline, just exquisite. He shuddered at the thought of touching her there, caressing that lovely neck and feeling the satisfying snap of her vertebrae. And then he'd have her, any way he wanted her, as many times as he wanted, the dirty little whore. It would be the best Christmas ever.

He drank his beer, left the money on the bar, with just enough of a tip to not be memorable, and waited outside in the rental van, pretending to be studying a map, until his Latin beauty left. He watched her get into an old Toyota pickup and when he was a block away, he pulled out and followed her through town.

A costume party. Perfect. Where else could he blend in, move among them, listen to their conversations, then wait for his moment, then take his prize, right under their noses? He was truly blessed, or cursed maybe, but cursed in a wonderful, wonderful way.

> *. . . Had a very shiny neck.*
> *And if you ever snapped it*
> *You would even say it . . . uh . . . glows.*

"Stupid song," he said.

"I think Val wants a Chinese baby," said Gabe Fenton. He was drinking beers with Tucker Case and Theo Crowe in the tower of the lighthouse on a limited-edition windless Tuesday before Christmas. They had lawn chairs set up where the light used to be and were watching a pod of dolphins playing in the bay below.

"For Christmas?" asked Tucker Case. "That seems like a pretty expensive gift. What do those things go for, ten—twenty grand?"

Theo gave Tuck a dirty look, which had never ceased being his reaction to the pilot, but sometime during the year, since it didn't appear that Tuck was going to go away, Theo and Gabe had accepted him as a friend.

"The question is," Theo said, "are you ready to be a parent?"

"Oh, she doesn't want to share it. She just wants one for herself. She says she couldn't stand to have me around the house all the time, because I live like an animal."

"Well, you are a biologist," said Tuck defensively. "It's kind of your work."

"Truth," said Gabe, raising his fist and offering the pilot a righteous pound for truth.

"Truth," said Tuck, taking and returning the pound (the more weighty, clinched version of the high five, generally less flamboyant than its open-palmed brother, but no less awkward when performed by geeky white guys. *Can you dig it? Right on.*).

Theo rolled his eyes and shoved a pretzel into the waiting Labrador retriever at his side. "She doesn't even like you, Gabe. You said so yourself."

"Yet she allows you regular boning privileges," said

Tuck. "That implies, oh, a certain lack of judgment on her part. I like that in a woman."

"She does smell nice," said Gabe.

"That's no reason to have a child with her," Theo said.

"Or buy her an expensive present," added Tuck.

"So what are you going to be at Lonesome Christmas?" asked Gabe, desperate now to change the subject.

"I'm thinking Pirate," Theo said. "I still have the eye patch from when I got conjunctivitis last summer."

"How about Law Man?" said Tuck, snickering.

"So what are you going as," asked Theo, "a human being?"

"I'm not going. I have to work," said Tuck.

"You dog!" said Gabe, "How did you manage that?"

At the mention of "dog," Skinner moved to the Food Guy's side, just in case there was a pretzel over there that he might be missing.

"Christmas Eve is a huge drug holiday. It's supposed to be cold tonight. We're going to fly around looking for heat signatures from meth labs. I'm hoping that some tweeker will put a newbie in charge of the cooking for the holiday and we'll get an explosion. Nothing says Christmas like a burning meth lab."

"Does Lena know?" Theo raised an eyebrow.

"Not yet. I'm going to get called in at the last minute."

"She'll be furious," Gabe said.

"You really should go," said Theo. "It's important to her."

"Maybe I'll show up late, forgo the costume. Women love it when they expect the usual disappointment, then at the last minute you surprise them with something romantic, like showing up."

"God, you're a weasel."

"What, I said I'm coming."

"Actually, weasels don't deserve the negative reputation they've acquired," said Gabe. "They are, in fact—"

"Do you think you could take Roberto?" Tuck said to Theo. "He could be, like, your pirate parrot."

"I hate costume parties," Gabe said. "It's as if you reveal your true nature through your costume, no matter how hard you try not to."

"So, Tuck," Theo said, "you should have a weasel costume lying around."

Mavis Sand believed that a truly great fruitcake should contain only enough fruit and flour as was required to get the pharmaceuticals to stick together. This year, that meant about a handful each of maraschino cherries and Gold Medal unbleached. She did break down at the last minute and use a half a cup of sugar, because the Xanax was adding a bitter aftertaste that fucked up the one-fifty-one rum burn. She'd also traded out drinks all night for twenty hits of Ecstasy (XTC) from a kid with a shaved and tattooed scalp and so many facial piercings that he looked as if he'd been bobbing for u-bolts in the nail bin at the hardware store. He felt pretty sure that the tabs were X, but even if they turned out to be animal tranquilizers, the party would be a success. Mavis had always disliked the teetotaling tone of the Lonesome Christmas and just wanted to see some people lose control in a church environment without trying to take any of her rights away.

Now, the afternoon of the party, the cake of oblivion had been cut into harmless-looking little cubes that nested in red and green waxed-paper candy cups, arranged on a silver tray like the petals of a friendly Christmas blossom. Mavis cackled to herself as she placed the last one, then went to start the oak wood in the barbecue behind the chapel.

"*Smell that?*" said Marty in the Morning (*all the dirt-nap hits that you wanna hear*). "We're talkin' barbecue, kids!"

"*Well, I for one thought that the lasagna last year was a mistake,*" said Bess Leander, who was suspicious of all food after having been poisoned by her husband. "*That's not Christmas party food. That's just lazy.*"

"*I do hope they sing 'Good King Wenceslas,'*" said Esther.

"*You're on the Wenceslas express, by request, with Marty in the Morning, right here on W-D-E-D, Dead radio for Pine Cove and the entire Central Coast.*"

"*You're not on the radio anymore, Marty,*" said Jimmy Antalvo.

"*I know that. You think I don't know that?*"

"*Hey, do you think the two docs will do it in the graveyard again this year?*" asked Jimmy, getting in the Christmas spirit.

"*Oh yes, we can only hope,*" said Malcolm Cowley, sarcastically. "*For I would love nothing more than to, once again, listen to the awkward gropings of lustful reprobates while banal Christmas carols drone in the background! Oh, be still my heart!*"

"*Good one, Malcolm,*" said Marty.

By that evening, when the party actually rolled around, the tri-tips were barbecued medium-rare and encrusted with rosemary and garlic, the punch bowl lay like a great Day-Glo pond among a field of potluck casseroles, salads, and hors d'oeuvres, and pieces of Mavis's fruitcake were lined up like tiny soldiers ready to march into the breech for the glory of Christmas, Country, and the Baby Jesus, Goddammit!

The partiers, once resistant to the idea of a costume Christmas, had finally surrendered and allowed themselves to revel in the humiliation of a festive defeat. Gabe Fenton had fashioned a killer whale costume out of papier-mâché and spray paint, but had forgotten to make flippers with sleeves, and instead was trapped in a black-and-white shell with his arms pinned down, his face inside the orca's mouth, covered with a black stocking with his glasses on the outside, giving the appearance that the killer whale had just eaten a biologist and was burping up the indigestible wire rims.

"Gabe, that you?" Theo asked.

"Yeah, how could you tell?"

"Well, your hiking books are showing under your tail, and I think you're the only one who would know the actual proportions of a killer whale penis."

"Yeah, they're prehensile," Gabe said. The pink appendage, nearly two feet long and as thin as a garden hose, whipped against Theo's leg. "They can actually do it around corners. I'm working it with a drain snake."

"That's lovely," Theo said, pushing back his ten-gallon hat. "Wait until you see Mavis's outfit. You guys should do a dance or something."

"So you're supposed to be a marshal, right?" asked Val Riordan, whose arm was intertwined with Gabe's limp flipper.

"Yeah, well, I had the badge," Theo said.

"I thought you were going to be a pirate," Gabe said.

Theo winced. "Turns out that Molly has some bad history with pirates."

"Sorry," Gabe said. "You guys fighting?"

Theo nodded dolefully.

"Is she here?" Val said, doing a little curtsy in antici-pation of showing off to Molly. Theo had been trying to avoid looking at the psychiatrist, but there she was, drawing attention to herself.

Valerie Riordan wore a black vinyl miniskirt and high spike-heeled red hooker boots, a silver crop-top see-through blouse with a plunging neckline, and external shoulder pads fashioned from the cerebral cortex lobes of the model plastic brain that used to grace the coffee table in her office. Down the outside of her right thigh she had henna-tattooed the words EGO, ID, and SUPER-EGO; down the other were the words DESIRE, DENIAL, and OBSESSION. Up the inside of her right thigh and disappearing under the micro-miniskirt was the word LUST; up the inside of the other thigh in equally provocative placement was the word GUILT. With the clever application of false eyelashes, glitter, too much rouge, and tramp-red lipstick, her makeup gave her an expression of perpetual surprise associated with inflat-able sex dolls.

"I'm a Mind Fuck," Val said.

"Yeah, but what's your costume?" Theo asked.

Theo heard a snort come out of the killer whale as the psychiatrist spun on a spiked heel and strutted toward the punch bowl.

"I'm going to pay for that," Gabe said.

"Sorry, spreading the misery," said Theo.

"It's okay. It was worth it."

Then Gabe paddled off to find Skinner, who was jingling around the room dressed as a reindeer. Theo cased the room for an estranged warrior babe.

Gabe encountered Estelle Boyette and Catfish Jefferson by a tray of cheese and crackers. Estelle, an artist in her sixties, had come as Mother Nature. She wore a diaphanous gown and had leaves and glitter fastened into her long gray hair. Flower petals were tacked to her face and arms with Superglue. She looked like what might have resulted if Stevie Nicks had mated with a Rose Bowl float. Her date, Catfish, the blues man, wore his usual leather fedora, his everyday gray sharkskin suit over a work shirt, and his usual gold tooth with the ruby chip in the middle. A single jingle bell hung on a silver thread from the neck of his National Steel guitar.

"What are you supposed to be?" Gabe asked.

"Cheerful."

"How would I know that?"

"Ain't wearin' my shades."

"Word," said Gabe.

"Don't do that."

"Sorry."

"Have some fruitcake," Mavis said to Lena, who was dressed as Snow White. Tucker Case had wanted to come as one of the Seven Dwarfs until Lena informed him that while Grumpy, Sneezy, and Dopey were indeed members of the original diminutive seven, Horny was not, and no amount of padding the package of his dwarf shorts was going to change that, so Tuck faked a call from the DEA on his cell and pretended to head off to work.

Mavis was manning the carving knife, slicing off great slabs of bloody beef and forking them onto the plates of passersby, whether they wanted them or not.

"I'm a vegetarian," said a woman who was dressed like a fairy.

"No, you're not. Eat it. You look like Death eating a cracker, and I know from Death, I been tossing his salad for twenty years just so I could keep drawing breath."

The woman scampered off, holding her roast beef like it was radioactive waste.

"Jeeze, Mavis," Lena said, pausing as she bit into a cube of the psychoactive confection.

"What? You make a deal, you follow through, right?"

Lena nodded, looking a little sad now. "You're supposed to."

"You got stood up?"

"He had to work."

"Dirtbag."

Just then a dashing version of Zorro appeared at Lena's side and offered her a glass of punch. "Refreshment, my lady," Zorro said.

"Thanks," Lena said, trying to figure out who was behind the mask. "The fruitcake is a little—" She shot a glance over her shoulder at Mavis, who brushed a long black hair out of her eyes. "—I'm a little parched."

"And our lovely hostess's costume is . . .?" asked Zorro.

"A burro with a dick like a whiffle-ball bat," Mavis growled, like it was perfectly obvious, especially since she'd sewn an actual whiffle-ball bat into the furry black costume.

"Of course," said Zorro. He grinned as he watched his Snow White drink the punch that he'd spiked with the powdered Rohypnol.

Oh, she was perfect, his little Latin Snow White. The Zorro costume had been a stroke of genius. He didn't even have to conceal the saw-toothed dagger that he used to take his trophies. There it hung, right on his belt next to the fake saber. He liked the feel of the tall Zorro boots as well. He was going to wear them while he had his way with her.

Just a few short steps out the back door, then through

the graveyard and the woods to his waiting van on the next block. If he played his cards right, no one would even see them leave. He checked his watch, figured five, maybe ten minutes at most.

"Would you like to dance?" he asked Lena. An eighties New Wave song blasted from the boom box.

She seemed reticent at first, looked down at her blue frock, as if she expected bluebirds to come to her with the answer.

"C'mon, it's Christmas Eve," William Johnson said. "Cheer up."

"Well, okay then," Lena said. And she let him lead her out into the center of the chapel.

The Warrior Babe of the Outland had come through the door with her sword drawn, wearing gunmetal armor that perfectly conformed to the curves of her body. Wicked spikes jutted from the forearms and shoulders and gauntlets, the helmet was crowned by a grinning gunmetal skull with ram horns. At the last minute, after her argument with Theo about whether his choice to dress as a pirate was made simply to irritate her, she'd decided to forgo any Christmas decorations. Instead, where her skin showed, at her midriff, face, and thighs, she'd painted herself shiny black with Kiwi shoe polish. If Satan had commissioned Smith & Wesson to build him a stripper, something that looked like Molly would be swinging on the headliner pole in Hell's Own Booty Lounge.

After a brief visit to the buffet table, where she'd wolfed down a pound of roast beef and a handful of fruitcake, she retreated to a spot by the Christmas tree, near the Nativity scene and the bat, and avoided making eye contact with her husband. Oh, she would forgive him before the night was through, she knew it, but first he would have to suffer.

That was before the fruitcake kicked in. When someone has the delicate constitution and borderline personality disorder of a Warrior Babe, medications do not always affect her in the same way they do others. A balanced cocktail of Xanax and XTC, which might induce a lazy euphoria in the average person, which was what Mavis had been banking on, instead sent Molly dipping into the guacamole of unreality, which first manifested in her finding the three wise men and the shepherds mildly threatening.

"I could take them," she said.

"Well, I hope so," said the bat, who was hanging upside down on the Christmas tree. Roberto had returned as General Douglas MacArthur, mostly because he shared with the dead general an affinity for aviator sunglasses, but also because Tuck had gotten a deal on a tiny corncob pipe and an officer's hat with the ear holes already cut out on eBay.

"They're only nine inches tall," the furry general pointed out, with just a hint of his Filipino accent.

"I mean if they were real, I could take them," said Molly, who was sure she saw the nearest king make a move for the frankincense.

"So have you seen Lena?" asked the bat, casually.

"No. I looked for her. She went with Snow White then? Tuck gave in on the dwarf?"

"Tuck's not here. She just left with another guy."

"You're kidding."

"She looked a little tipsy."

"Lena doesn't drink."

"That's not how it looked."

"Should I go find her?"

"She's your friend. Would you grab me one of those pineapple slices if you pass the buffet table?"

"Get it yourself. You can fly."

"I would, but that donkey with the giant schlong kinda freaks me out."

"Okay, I see your point there," said the Warrior Babe, not at all nonplussed that she was talking to a flying mammal who was smoking a pipe.

"What's it doing with the killer whale?"

William led Lena to a tall monument in the middle of graveyard and leaned her against it.

"Oh, poo," said Lena, noticing that she'd gotten some dirt on her Snow White dress. Her head lolled a little, then she giggled. "Not Snow White anymore."

The drugs had done their work, but she was more alert than his Christmas treats usually were. Still helpless, but more awake. That would be good. Really good. As long as she didn't scream.

"Just be still," William said. He put his hand on her throat and pinned her to the monument. He thought, given her level of alertness, that he should take her to the van to finish this part, but she was so hot, so deserving. And when would he get another chance to be Zorro in a graveyard?

He pulled his knife from the sheath just as he lost his grip on Lena and she slid down the gravestone to a sitting position.

"Oops," she said.

Why was she still talking? They were never talking at this point. He'd seen her drinking some coffee earlier in the evening while eating some fruitcake, but one cup of coffee shouldn't counteract the dose that he'd put in her punch.

"Tuck loves me. He can't help it he's a rascal," Lena said.

"Shut up, bitch." William thumped her on the head with the butt of the knife, and when she opened her mouth to say ouch, he grabbed her tongue between his fingers and pulled.

Strange. Amid all the amazing sensations that were nearly driving him into a frenzy—the feel of her tongue, her skin, her hair, the knife, the anticipation—among them he thought he smelled the odor of shoe polish. Strange.

"Thi, Tha tha," said Lena, by which she meant, "Hi, Molly," but, of course, there was a serial killer holding on to her tongue so she wasn't enunciating as crisply as usual.

The killer looked around and something cold and very sharp pressed against his cheek. He felt the skin break and blood run down his neck.

"Let go of her tongue," said the black apparition before him. All he could really see was a long blade that disappeared into gunmetal outlines around the shadow of a woman. He let go of Lena's tongue and flipped the knife around so it was hidden by his forearm.

"Up," said the shade. She kept the blade against his cheek as he stood up, which hurt like hell. He kept his knife hand at his side and waited.

"Ouch," said Lena. "Molly, I'm not feeling good. Fruitcake, I think." She tried to stand and tumbled off to the side of the gravestone.

Molly stepped past the killer to try to catch her, and

that's when he made his move, bringing the knife up in a quick arc toward her chest.

Molly felt a sharp blow against her sternum, heard a sharp crack, then swung around with the sword at neck level, but as she came around, the killer was already falling. She saw a tiny red flower blooming on his forehead as he hit the ground, his eyes wide to the stars. Coming out of the mist, with light from the chapel window throwing a halo around his head and shoulders, was a tall drink of water in a ten-gallon hat, a Glock 9mm held at his side.

"You guys okay?" Theo said. "I told you that costumes make people act weird."

Molly looked at the dent in her armor, the black finish marred and showing the steel plate beneath it. She grinned at the Constable, and in the dark, painted black, she appeared very much like the Cheshire Cat. "Oh yeah, that was the problem: his outfit."

"Where is she? What happened?"

"Hey, everybody, check it out," said Jimmy Antalvo. *"A new guy."*

"Hey, new guy," said Marty in the Morning. *"I'm Marty, coming to you direct from Pine Cove, with all the hits you love to push up daisies to."*

"*Where—where am I?*" asked William Johnson. "*It's dark.*"

"*You're deceased, you imbecile,*" said Malcolm Cowley, who hated change, along with most other things.

"*Oh, a new fellow,*" said Esther. "*How exciting. Do you know the words to 'Good King Wenceslas'?*"

Molly and Mavis ministered to Lena, giving her coffee and sympathy over by the piano, while, over by the front doors, Theo explained what had happened to a brace of detectives from the sheriff's department. They'd already found William Johnson's van, with the various instruments of torture and the blister pack of human tongues, so the consensus was that Theo was going to be regarded as a hero, which irritated them to no end.

An emergency medical technician had taken a look at Lena, pronounced her healthy but definitely wasted, and recommended that she go to the hospital just to be safe, but she would not leave, insisting that Tucker Case would come to get her. And a few minutes later, as Mavis was reminding Molly for the thirty-seventh time that she was, in fact, a retired actress and not the Warrior Babe of the Outland, and therefore not duty-bound by a blood oath to take the man in the ten-gallon hat home and have sex with him until neither of them could walk, Tucker Case walked through the doors.

"What happened?" asked the pilot. He was dressed as Amelia Earhart, curls from a blond wig peeking out from under a leather flying helmet and goggles, wearing a silk scarf, riding boots, and jodhpurs, and a big badge with wings on it that declared "Amelia Earhart" in big brass letters, just in case someone missed the other clues.

"Tuck," cried Lena, and she ran into his arms. "I knew you'd come."

"Yeah, well, you know, I thought about it . . ."

"And you missed me?" She sort of slid down the front of him.

"Are you—uh—Lena, are you intoxicated?"

"I'm sorry. I had a bad night."

"No, it's okay. My bad. I should have been here?"

"A serial killer tried to cut her tongue out," said Mavis, casually, brushing a donkey ear away from her eye. "Theo shot him."

"Wow. Okay, then, I'm not the villain of this story," said Tuck.

"You're my hero," said Lena, sort of oozing to the floor.

"Can one of you guys help me get her to the car?" Tuck asked Molly and Mavis.

"Sure," said Molly, pulling her friend to her feet and bracing her under her shoulder while Tuck took the other side. "Why Amelia Earhart?"

"You know, the pilot thing. And I was hoping for

some hot girl-on-girl action under the Christmas tree if Lena forgave me."

"That would be lovely," said Lena.

Tuck blinked. "Okay, let's get her to the car." He looked over his shoulder to Mavis, nodding to her sewn-on appendage. "Nice unit there, Mavis."

"Right back atcha, flyboy," said Mavis.

And as Amelia Earhart and Kendra, the Warrior Babe of the Outland, assisted the heavily medicated Snow White to her car, and a Mind Fuck with an MD shagged a killer whale with a PhD on the grave of a DJ back in the cemetery, General Douglas MacArthur, the fruit bat, flew to the top of the Christmas tree, did a half-swing around it as he grabbed the star, and said:

"Merry Christmas to all, and to all a good night."

Author's Note

Some of the characters that appeared in *The Stupidest Angel* have also appeared in my previous novels. Raziel, the stupidest angel, appeared in *Lamb: The Gospel According to Biff, Christ's Childhood Pal*. Theophilus Crowe, Molly Michon, Gabe Fenton, and Valerie Riordan all appeared in *The Lust Lizard of Melancholy Cove*. Robert Masterson, Jenny Masterson, and Mavis Sand appeared both in *Practical Demonkeeping* and *The Lust Lizard of Melancholy Cove*. Tucker Case and Roberto the Fruit Bat appeared in *Island of the Sequined Love Nun*.